D1596647

Northward to Home

JUST JOHN, BOOK 2

NORTHWARD TO HOME

REG QUIST

THORNDIKE PRESS
A part of Gale, a Cengage Company

Copyright © 2021 Reg Quist.
Thorndike Press, a part of Gale, a Cengage Company.

Thorndike Press® Large Print Hardcover Western.
The text of this Large Print edition is unabridged.
Other aspects of the book may vary from the original edition.
Set in 16 pt. Plantin.

LIBRARY OF CONGRESS CIP DATA ON FILE.
CATALOGUING IN PUBLICATION FOR THIS BOOK
IS AVAILABLE FROM THE LIBRARY OF CONGRESS.

ISBN-13: 979-8-8857-8168-8 (hardcover alk. paper)

Published in 2022 by arrangement with Wolfpack Publishing LLC.

Printed in Mexico
Print Number : 1   Print Year : 2023

FOREWORD

Just John, Book One, is fiction based on the few facts that are known about John Ware's early life. His travels follow the easier and most probable routes from South Carolina to Fort Worth, Texas. There is no record of how John got to Fort Worth or what events transpired along the way. All that is known is that he worked for several years as a cowboy on at least two Fort Worth ranches before signing on with the trail herd that brought him north. *Just John* invents an interesting scenario to fill in his lost travel experiences.

Book Two, *Northward to Home* is historical, based on the few recorded and known facts of John Ware's life. John himself was illiterate. He left no known records of his history or thoughts. To fill in the gaps in the story that were not recorded in history, the author has taken the liberty to create the possible details, in keeping with the culture

5

and traditions of the era. *Northward to Home* is not intended to be taken as a totally accurate biography because no such biographical or background information exists. But the important events that were historically recorded by his friends and family, several years after his death, are faithfully transferred into the narrative. Some events recorded by others and claimed as historical, the author finds suspect, and not worthy of repetition.

There is nothing in this telling of the story that intentionally distorts the John and Millie Ware story.

We hope you enjoy this historical western.

CHAPTER 1

Tom Lynch stood in his stirrups and waved his Stetson over his head, trying to gain John's attention. But it was Clayton Burgess who saw the wave and lifted his hat while staring across the herd, in effect asking a question. Tom pointed his hat at John, barely visible through the dust cloud and the rising heat waves off the backs of the sweating cattle. Clayton dipped his hat in understanding. He turned in his saddle. A shrieking whistle sounded through his teeth and over his curled lips, a sound that gained John's attention, but also a sound that Tom feared would one day cause the herd to rise into a run.

When John looked up, Clayton pointed across the backs of three thousand dusty, sweating animals. It was only then that the black rider understood. Waving his own hat, John pulled off to the side, from his flank position, and waited for the tail end of the herd to pass him by.

As the last drag rider, enveloped in dust and sweat and cow stink, rode past him, John kicked his horse into motion, riding wide of the herd and the other crewmen. In a couple of minutes, he pulled up beside Tom, who was sitting with one leg hooked over the horn, while his cigarette smoke rose into the dusty air.

Initially, Tom had refused to take this black man onto the drive crew. He had no faith in any black man's riding ability, or his handling of horses or cattle. It was only when Bill Moodie made himself clear to Tom, that the trail driver relented. Tom had wanted Bill, a well experienced drover, and a widely respected man. He nodded his approval with the condition, "I'll give him a few days to prove up. I'll not have a man that leaves his load for others to carry."

Since that day John had shown himself to be the equal of any man on the drive.

"John, you see that pile of rocks over there?"

"Yassir, Boss. What dat be for? Why someone take de time ta pile de rocks up out here on dis grass?"

"Have you ever seen a map of the country, John? I mean the whole country, top to bottom and side to side."

8

"No sir, Boss, I ain't never seen no map like dat."

"Where are you from originally, John? I'm assuming you were a slave on some farm or plantation."

"Yassir, I be slave down to Sout' Carolina. Big farm. Left from outa der 'n rode my ol' Hound-Dog horse to Tennessee. Hound Dog, he up an' die of old age back down de Montana trail, short time back.

"Worked on de horse ranch fo' more dan one year befo' rid'n wit some fok's to Fort Worth. Dat be down to Texas. I be in Fort Worth past one year. Den go ride fo' Mr. Tubbs. He own de "T" ranch down der. Stay der maybe-so five years. Rancher, he be kep me on fo' to work de cattle 'n de horses. Mostly de horses. Gentle and train fo' rid'n and fo' pull'n de wagon. Rancher, he sell de horses down to Fort Worth."

"So how did you get up here? To Montana?"

"I be work'n fo' 'nother ranch. Mr. Blandon, he own de XX. Small place wit jest de two riders. Fella named Bo an Ol' John. Boss man Blandon, he raise de runn'n horses. Racehorses, he call dem. Raise cow critters too but mostly he love de horses.

"I be work'n der three years, train'n de horses and chas'n de cows, time ta time.

Den, I be want'n ta see mo' o' de country, Boss. Maybe-so find other way ta make money for ta buy my own ranch someday. Maybe-so make more dan de ranch wages. I ride wit' de herd. Go to place be call Dodge City. Den we take 'nother herd ta place be call Cheyenne. Dat be in Wyoming. Big place. Lots a people, maybe-so near as big as Fort Worth. Too much crowded. Ol' John not want'n ta stay. Ride wit Bill Moodie tak'n 'nother herd to dis Montana place.

"Bill Moodie, he say we go ta de gold mine. Maybe-so we make much money. Mor' dan fo herd'n de cows."

John chuckled at his last statement while Tom smiled at the remembrance of the story with the unhappy ending that Bill, himself, had told.

"Well, John, you've seen more of these United States than I have. I've seen maps of the whole area though. The country is very large. But although it's a big land, it doesn't just keep on going and going. Mexico hangs tight on the southern border and the oceans wash up to the east and west coasts. On the north is Canada. Some years ago, the surveyors worked their way across this vast land and staked out the borders. They marked that border from east to west for thousands of miles. Sometimes they placed iron peg markers into solid rock. I'm told that's what they did in those high up Rocky Mountains we're following, off there to the west just a short bit.

"But on the grasslands," Tom continued, pointing to the large stack of rounded prairie boulders, placed in a rough square about four feet to a side on the ground and rising to a single balanced rock at the top, about four feet above the surrounding grass, "Where there is no rock to hold an iron peg securely, they piled up what's called a rock cairn. They might pile the rocks around an iron peg driven into the black loam or they may stand a wooden post up and pile the rock around it.

"What you're looking at there is a rock cairn, marking the border between the United States and Canada. Right now, sitting here, you and I are still in the United States. The herd has moved on into Canada. And that's where we're going."

"Where we tak' dis herd, Boss?"

"We're taking them to Fort Macleod. That's just a little over one hundred miles. We'll be there in less than a week."

"What be dis Fort Macleod place?"

"Fort Macleod is a small village, but it's where the Canadian police make their headquarters. They're called the North-

11

West Mounted Police."

Tom dropped his foot back into the stirrup and nudged his horse into a walk. John rode along beside him, turning just once to look back at the rock cairn. The herd was walking in a tight group, showing no stragglers. John wouldn't be needed for another few minutes.

"The North-West Mounted Police, the NWMP, as they're known, were set up by the Canadian federal government to police the western half of the country. It seems the government, even from their comfortable offices, way down east, could see that they needed a police force on a land this big, before large numbers of settlers started arriving. The Hudson's Bay Company has administered the land for the past couple of hundred years. They kept the peace between natives and the Bay men pretty well too. There wasn't much out here but Bay men. Them and another company. But those two formed themselves into one company a long time ago. There were no free trappers or traders. For the most part the Indians did the trapping, and the Bay bought their furs. And that, too, turned out to be good for the Indians. So, everyone was more or less happy.

"But the Indian Tribes were constantly

battling with each other, creating many deaths on both sides. Then the American whiskey traders started causing serious problems. The Indians had never tasted whiskey but once they got ahold of the stuff they wanted more and more. It was ruining many lives.

"So, the NWMP was put together and sent out here, just a few years ago. By the time they arrived the whiskey traders had all left. And slowly, the Indians have stopped fighting each other. I suspect the distance between their villages, and having the Mounties riding the land, helps considerably with that. Mostly now, or so I'm told, the Bands are staying close to their own recognized territories.

"This grass couldn't stay unused forever. We're among the first to bring cattle in and I must say, it's mighty nice to bring cows into a land that's organized and policed and not ruled with a six-gun.

"The farmers and townsmen will follow along, but that won't happen until the railway is finished. That will take some time yet.

"The Canadian government felt it was better to form up a special police force, rather than send out the army. They've been proven to be correct on that. In the entire history of the world, I doubt if there has ever been an army that either made peace or held the peace. That's not what armies do.

"The settlements up here are not policed by local sheriffs like they are down south. The NWMP have taken on the task. Done a pretty good job of it too, although there are mighty few real settlements. Gun fights and violence are almost unknown.

"Unfortunately, none of that means the Indians are being treated well or fairly but so far, the Mounties have pretty well held it together."

John seemed to think on this information for a few seconds before turning to Tom.

"I's be goi'n' back to da job now, Boss. Maybe-so we talk again bout dis Canada place."

"Maybe-so we will, John."

As John turned to leave, Tom called him back.

"There's one more thing, John. It doesn't particularly matter to me, but it will matter to some. Pretty much everyone has a second, or family name. You have chosen to be known as just John. But the Mounties may wish to know your other name. It's not easy, what with all the riders moving about, but they do what they can to know who is in the country. And I'm pretty sure Mr. Stimson, the man we're delivering these cattle to, will want to know more about you if you should decide to stay and work for him.

"Is there a good reason for you not speaking your other name?"

John, avoiding Tom's eyes while looking at nothing particular himself, lifted his sweat-soaked hat off his head and twisted it in his strong hands, a move that had become an almost automatic response to anything he found troubling. He had a family name. Although he didn't really know the history of the name, and his parents, more accepting of their slavery than he was himself, had never bothered to discuss the matter.

John had always thought of it as a slave name. A name assigned by his owner to identify and separate his family from the other slave families. He wasn't totally sure that his long-held belief was even the truth, but he had put the name behind him anyway, the day he rode away from the Shady Acres Farm, all those years ago. With time and maturity healing many of the old hurts and remembering that his father had willingly adopted the name, perhaps it was time to carry it again himself. He made a quick decision, not having given it much thought, and knowing that the name, once spoken, would be his forever.

Ignoring Tom's last question about having a reason for not using the name John simply said, "Ware, Boss. De family on de slave farm be known as Ware. I be John Ware."

As he turned to ride back to the herd, he was struggling with emotions he didn't really understand. But with a random medley of old hurtful images of slavery, and of the lost family he missed so much, forcing themselves through his mind, he crossed behind the drag riders and took up his flank position again.

Ware. The name given to his family. John. The name given by his parents. He was John Ware. And so, he would ever be known.

CHAPTER 2

A week later, the herd was gathered on untouched grass a few miles west of Fort Macleod, along the Oldman River. Tom Lynch named off three men to stay with the animals while the rest went to town. Gathering the town-bound group together they were given clear instructions before they left the bed-grounds camp.

"Men, if you're packing a weapon, take it off and leave it in camp. You'll have no need for it here, and it can bring you nothing but grief. Have a drink if you wish but don't start any trouble. Fella named Harry Taylor runs the hotel and bar. Known as Kamoose Taylor. Don't know where the name came from. Don't matter. What matters is that you understand he runs the place with an iron hand. Won't put up with anyone thinking to show how big or tough a man he is. Kamoose is a tough enough man himself.

"Mr. Fred Stimson owns these animals.

He's planning to meet up with us here. We'll be moving on towards his ranch site after the brutes have had a couple of days rest. Mr. Stimson is a big man. And loud. Friendly enough when circumstances warrant. If he's reached here by now, you'll know his voice without being told who it is. He enjoys a good time as much as any man. He'll likely join you in a drink. Might even slap you on the back for a job well done, getting the herd safely this far. But he'll tolerate no foolishness. You speak out of turn or cause a problem; you'll find yourself without a job.

"Don't go to thinking Fort Macleod is like any trail-side gathering of shacks you might have whooped it up in down south. It ain't the same at all.

"And try to keep in mind that Fort Macleod is the western headquarters for the North-West Mounted Police. There's more than just a few of them stationed here, although they're known for long rides into the far reaches of the country, so some of them may be out on patrol. But there's always a few around. Good men. Understanding of frontier ways. Tolerant, to a point. You don't want to venture past that point."

Tom waited for the few grumbling voices

to quiet before saying, "Now, we ain't likely to be asked to join no pink tea party with fancy, highborn ladies waving the heat away with little folding fans, since no such exist anywhere near here. But just the same, you'll want to be made welcome by whoever you meet. And that ain't going to be easy right at this exact time. To be truthful about it, you stink. I'm sure I do too. A bath and a cold-water wash of your clothing wouldn't cause any of you any lasting harm."

Pointing off to the north Tom said, "Now that over there, right down there in the bottom of that river valley, that's water. Good for drinking or, when the need is upon you, for having an all-over wash. I'd like if you would all follow me down there. It's a warm day. Between the sun and the wind, your clothing will dry out before we reach town, so give them a good scrub. Now mount up. Let's clean ourselves up and go to town."

Figuring his horse could benefit from the loss of some of the trail dust gathered in the past couple of weeks, John stripped the saddle and led the faithful gelding into the shallows along the Oldman River. The other riders were hanging back, waiting. What they were waiting for was unclear to Tom Lynch, who was already stripped to his long johns.

"You boys coming in or do I have to rope you and drag you in?"

Clink Mohan laughed and answered, "Heard about quicksand up this way. I'm waiting to see just what happens with you and John. You start to sink, you let me know when you want me to rope you out'a there. I ain't set'n out to spoil yer fun."

Without turning around John answered, "No quicksand here, Boss. Jes nice warm water heated by this here prairie sun. Why, it mus' be twenty, maybe even thirty mile this here water rolled across de grass land since it melted off'en dat ice pack you can see over to da west. Any warmer I couldn't stand it."

With that, John struggled out of the long johns he had cut the legs off and stepped into deeper water. He splashed water over the horse's back as best he could with no rag, nor a bucket close to hand. He figured the horse could do the rest himself. The un-named horse, known as the herd outlaw before John managed to partially tame him, had no idea how to respond to the show of kindness. John narrowly missed a swinging hind hoof before moving aside to scrub his clothing while keeping an eye on the big gelding, hoping he wouldn't decide to return to Idaho.

Clink, taking a long look at John as he sat in the shallows along the river's edge, with the water just reaching his waist, said, "John, I ain't never seen you with no shirt on before. Judging by looks alone, I'd say at the next river crossing you could carry these beeves across, one under each arm. I ain't never seen no man built so much like a bull as you. I ever need something lifted I can't manage myself, I'll surely give you a call."

John could find no suitable response, so he said nothing.

Although every man who cared to look could see the whip scars on John's back, out of shock, and respect for their black riding mate, no one chose to comment.

Clink stripped down, rolled his clothes into a bundle and carried them into the water. As the river rose towards his waist, he let out a 'whoo-ee' that could be heard back at the camp.

"Dang, John, here I was saying just the other day what an honorable and trustworthy fella you was. Now, I find you ain't told the exact whole truth of how warm this water is. Why, a good camp cook could make coffee directly from the river and save the need for boil'n 'er up. C'mon in you fellas, this here is downright pleasant."

With much yelping as the glacier melt

water threatened to turn lips blue and cause uncontrollable shivering on the seldom washed bodies of the riders, along with good-natured teasing, the baths and clothes washing were completed and the ride to town resumed.

The crew tied their horses at the railing in front of Kamoose Taylor's Hotel Fort Macleod, a chinked-log affair housing the hotel and eating house, along with a bar and gambling room.

"Welcome boys. Welcome to the finest hotel establishment in this here entire country. Beds, good food, and if your desires should run that way, perhaps a mild tonic to cut the memory of the dusty miles put behind you.

"We have an agreement here we would ask you to sign on to boys. You agree to make no ruction and pay your bill when asked, and I agree to not break your head open with a bung starter or a bottle, that could be put to better use if opportunity should provide. Now if that sounds fair enough to you, c'mon in and enjoy yourselves."

This was all said with a smile and a broad Isle of Wight accent, that hadn't lessened one bit during his years in Canada. Nor did the smile thin down the seriousness of the

22

warning welcome.

Tom led the crew inside and into the drinking portion of the establishment. They found chairs and gathered them around a single table, seating themselves in their still damp clothing. Within a minute, Kamoose himself approached carrying a bottle and a handful of small glasses. If anyone in the room noticed John's color, no one mentioned it.

From his first experience of rejection, during his years-ago travels on behalf of the farmer who owned him, acceptance into the larger society had become a growing familiarity for John. As more black men joined the ranks of ranch riders, becoming, over time, fully accepted cowboys, the rejection had become almost a thing of the past, on the ranches, if not in the towns.

John knew from his time in Cheyenne and Fort Worth, that the races and cultures of the larger towns and cities tended towards separation. At least, more so than in the new and scattered villages of a growing West.

Tom Lynch left the group and went looking for Fred Stimson. There weren't many places to look in the village, and the rancher was finally located at the NWMP barracks. Besides saying hello to a few old acquaintances, Stimson wanted some assurances on

23

the situation with the Blackfoot tribe.

"We're delivering a big herd to the ranch James. I'd like some assurance that the food rations for the Tribe will be met without my unwilling benevolence. We simply can't afford the loss of our breeding animals."

The officer, James Hyer, although well-known to Fred from previous visits, could only stumble an answer.

"We do what we can do, Fred. But you already know that. This is a big country. We can't be everywhere all the time. Anyway, with the Blackfoot, it's more than just the food. It's the land. And it's the culture. We may somehow convince ourselves that they're happy and content on the reserve. But, of course, that's not true and isn't likely to become true.

"The buffalo are gone and the men who used to spend each summer and fall on the hunt are now sitting around the reserve eating beef gifted to them by the government. They have no way to prove their manliness or provide for their families. And as to being proven a great warrior, that's pretty much a thing of the past. They aren't happy about that either.

"I suspect that from time to time they saddle up and cross into Montana. What goes on down there is not my problem. Of course, our patrolling officers have seen a goodly number of Sioux horses in Blackfoot villages, which makes us wonder. We don't ask. That way they don't have to lie to us.

"Taking one of your beefs is in no way the equivalent of riding down a buffalo, but I can't promise it won't happen.

"We'll do our best for you. But you're one of the first on the grass in this area and the very first to go that far west. You'll have to keep your riders out and scouting too.

"But let me remind you, any vigilante action taken will be met with the full force of the law. We won't tolerate it. You might want to remind your crew of that."

Stimson was about to make a loud reply when he spotted Tom Lynch approaching. Putting off any further discussion with the officer, he leaped to his feet.

"Tom. Am I glad to see you, man! May I assume the herd is somewhere close by?"

"Close enough, Fred. Most of the boys are over wetting down the dust they've swallowed. Why don't you come have a sip with them?"

"I'll do just exactly that, and I'll gladly buy, as well."

Turning to the officer he said, "Thanks for your time and advice, James. Trust me when I say I have listened and will take it all to heart."

As Tom and Fred were making their way back to the hotel, Stimson spotted a familiar man coming their way. Too far away to recognize the face, he was still easily identified by his bowlegged walk and his unusual hat that topped off the fringed buckskin jacket that hung over his leather pants which, in turn were tucked into his knee-high leather moccasins.

"Jerry. Jerry Potts. You old scoundrel. I'd a thought you'd be caught up and married off to some likely maiden by this time. Some girl looking to partake of the finer portions of life on this frontier."

Not bothering to reply to the foolishness cast his way by the boisterous Stimson, Jerry swung his 1866 Winchester Lever Action Yellowboy into his left hand and shook Stimson's hand with a small smile.

"You back to stay, Stimson? I see a herd outside town, off to the west. They yours?"

"Those will surely be mine. I doubt that there's another herd on the grass yet. But there soon will be if my guess turns out to be correct.

"Jerry, I want you to meet Tom Lynch, my drive boss. Tom, this is Jerry Potts. He's been here for so long; it's said he watched as those mountains rose from the ground.

26

There's no one anywhere around that understands this west better than Jerry Potts. And that's a fact. He's a good man to know."

As Lynch and Potts were shaking hands and judging each other with keen eyes, Stimson said, "We're just now heading over to the hotel to meet the crew and dampen down the dust. Will you join us, Jerry?"

Turning to walk beside the rancher, Potts said, "I believe I will. Just for a short bit, mind you. I've got to meet a man. Of course, he was expecting me yesterday, so I guess another few minutes' delay won't stop the grass from growing."

Pulling chairs over to the table that the crew was seated around, Tom said, "Fred, I'm guessing you met all of these men back in Montana."

As Stimson and the crew were nodding their acquaintance Tom said, "Fellas, you need to say hello to Mr. Jerry Potts. Jerry's an old timer around here, so I'm told. I'm also told he's a good man to know."

After Potts nodded at each man when their names were spoken, he held his eyes on John.

"John, is it? Well, John, I seen some few colored fellas working the Missouri boats, down at Fort Benton. Both slave and free on them river boats, back some years ago. Hard workers. Roustabouts mostly. Loading and unloading. Cutting and hauling fire-wood. That kind of thing.

"Mostly they had a rough go of it, but times have changed some. You're the first I've seen in these parts. You'll do alright. I'm a breed myself. Father's a Scot's fur trader. Mother a Kanai. That's a branch of the Cree. Named me Ky-yo-kose. Means Bear Child.

"Out here a man's judged on who he proves to be, John. Do your work. Keep your word. Show that you're trustworthy. Dependable. A riding partner that proves to be untrustworthy out here can be the death of a man. You'll get just the one chance to prove yourself."

With a boisterous laugh, Bill Moodie said, "Well, I guess you'd have to say John proved himself on one matter anyway."

Curious, Fred Stimson asked, "Yes? And what was that?"

"Why, wasn't a one of us, excepting me, that is, that knew John was a rider, and a good one too. Tom wasn't sure, at first, what work to trust John with, so he gave him an old horse and an older saddle and put him on night herd, and camp roustabout duties. John never complained, just being happy to be working and seeing new country. But finally, he'd had about enough of both saddle and horse. He comes to Tom, and he says, "I appreciates the job an' all Boss, but do you suppose I might get a bit better saddle and a bit worse hoss?"

The gathered men laughed at the remembrance, so Bill repeated the short punchline; "A bit better saddle and a bit worse hoss."

By this time every man in the room was focused on the storyteller.

"Well, as you can imagine fer your own selves, in a remuda of near a hundred cayuses, there's bound to be good and bad and about everything in between. So, when Tom agreed to what John asked for, the boys roped out this big grey that no one had been able to top off. Misery on four hoofs, that animal. Had more twists and turns a-com'n outa his feet than the most devious woman ever thought up fer ta confound her man.

"Well, they tied this brute down and managed to get the leather strapped in place. John, he tugged his hat down tight and put his foot in the stirrup. The boys let 'em go jest as John was swinging his leg over. Well sir, that ol' leather rose up to meet him and the ride was on. Why, you ain't never seen such a show. John wasn't even settled down yet, nor found the off-side stirrup when the leather rose up to smack the seat of his pants. But that grey, he was already under way with every evil move ever learned, and a few new ones recently thought up. A whole one pound can of black powder never exploded more than that there grey done. His four feet left the ground, and he twisted every which way. He hunched his spine and turned around so's to be pointed back to where he started from, landing with all four feet stiff to the sod. And that was just the start'n of the entertainment.

"John sat up there a whoop'n an' a holler'n and wav'n his one arm in the air and smil'n from ear to ear. With his strong legs wrapped tight to that cayuse, why he hardly left the saddle at all. That seemed to anger that outlaw all the more. Pretty soon he puts in to runn'n. When John got him turned back to the drive grounds, he came near to scatter'n the herd from one end of Idaho to the other, with John never mov'n from the leather.

"It started seem 'n like that grey wasn't ever going to quit, with first his heels point'n to the clouds and then revers'n, with his head swung back and his eyes glazed over. And then he took in to run again. But after a long run, to where we couldn't see neither beast nor rider, for dust and distance, here comes John back, sitt'n the saddle jest as calm as a mill pond duck, and that grey with his head hang'n, and sweat'n from every part of him.

"John, he rides back up to where we was all gap'n at the show and he says to Tom, 'This be a pretty good horse Mr. Lynch. I shore be lik'n if you'd let me keep dis here animal fer my own.' "

The men laughed as Bill attempted to copy John's mangled use of the language.

"Well, when Tom got over his surprise, he says, "John, if you want that horse, he's yours to ride. And to keep too, if you want him. Ain't no one else either wants him or what can ride him. I don't know as I've ever seen the likes of that ride. That's sure enough your horse. And the saddle too."

The table was silent for a moment as the men who had witnessed the ride waited to see the reaction to the story from Stimson and Potts.

Stimson simply reached over and gave a swat to John's shoulder that would have folded a lesser man over, while Jerry Potts grinned with no words offered.

When the table settled down again Potts turned to Stimson.

"You still determined to ranch up in

Blackfoot country?"

That simple question dominated the next hour's discussion. The riders left Lynch, Stimson and Potts to sort out the wisdom of ranching in new country and moved into the eating room.

CHAPTER 3

With a two-day rest behind them, the herd was pushed back onto the trail. From the Fort northward, towards the fledgling village of Fort Calgary, started by the NWMP, just like Fort Macleod had been, there was a winding, two-track, freight wagon and stagecoach trail through the untouched grass. No other travelers were encountered until a bull train of freight wagons heading back south presented itself. With the herd straddling the two-track, the riders attempted to claim priority over the trail. They didn't move until it became evident that the drivers of the bull train had no intention of giving way. The lead bulls and the drover riding along beside them were almost into the faces of the lead cattle before the herd split. With neither a nod nor a wave, the rider urged his bulls forward.

Several hundred head of cattle ran in fear, giving the cattlemen more excitement and work than they had planned on. With un-canny accuracy, the bull driver managed to spit a brown wad onto the legs of the drag rider's horse as that man was frantically pushing the last of the cows off the trail.

The crew lost an hour pulling the herd back together, before moving on towards the village known as The Crossing. For those who were unfamiliar with bull trains and the plodding determination of oxen, the lesson was learned.

The Crossing, being an as yet unfulfilled dream of a village, was attempting to rise from the roughhewn stopping place put together by the partners Smith and French, on the banks of the Highwood River.

After a brief rest stop at the Crossing, the herd was turned to the west, towards the glacier-topped Rockies, towards Blackfoot Territory and towards the leased land of the North West Cattle Company–the Bar U.

A single, unfinished log structure wel-comed the crew as they approached their final location. On their arrival, the cattle were turned loose on un-grazed Alberta grass. The Bar U was home and in business.

Fred Stimson called Tom Lynch aside with a question.

"Tom, we're going to need a crew. It's late in the season to be putting this herd on grass in an unfamiliar country, but here we are. We have it to do, is all. But we wouldn't want to be caught short handed. I've just a couple of men here now. Are there any of the drive crew that I should be bringing on?"

Tom didn't have to give the matter long thought. He easily answered, "I don't know how many men you want but you should keep Bill Moodie and John, if they'll stay. You'd ride a long way and sift the bushes down to their roots before you'd find two better men. Either man can work cattle responsibly and well, but if you need a man to put with the horses, John's the one you want."

The two men closed out their brief conversation after a few more names were noted by Stimson.

Fred called the men aside as they were gathering towards the chuckwagon for their first feeding on Bar U range.

"Listen up for a minute, men. I need a crew that will stay the winter. Now there may be one or two of you that can feel the home fires warming their bones and hear the old folks calling their names. I understand that and I wish you fair travelling. But for those that want to stay on, you've got a job on the Bar U. How many can I

35

count on?"

Several men glanced around the gathering to see what others were doing before committing themselves. Finally, one man said, "This is good looking country, and the drive went as well as any I've ever ridden with. If I didn't have a girl back in Idaho I'd sure enough sign on. But sorry, Boss. I'll be pulling out first thing in the morning."

Two others said they would also be riding south. The rest signed on with a simple nod, a mumbled, 'count me in', or an 'I'll stick with the brand'.

John said nothing, waiting to see if Mr. Stimson would call him out. He was also waiting for a signal from his friend Bill Moodie. When neither of those things happened, Tom Lynch took a hand, saying, "John, you haven't spoken yet." The question was left wrapped up in the short statement.

"Well, Boss. I guess ol' John would lak ta stay and work fer dis here Bar-U ranch. A's shore enough would. Bill and me, we's been rid'n together fo a long time. That job open fer Bill too?"

Tom grinned, remembering that it was Bill who had insisted he hire this black man when he didn't really want to. He spoke for Fred Stimson, assuming the obvious.

"I'm sure the Bar-U can use you both, John. What say you, Bill?"

One of the other men hollered out, "Make up your minds, fellas, that dinner wait'n over there ain't get'n no better, the longer it sits."

Bill glanced towards John and then to Fred Stimson before saying, "I think you can depend on John and me to make good hands for the winter."

Fred clapped his hands as if in relief.

"Good then let's call that done. And for you men who plan to ride home, thanks for the good work. I wish you well in the future. And now, just one more thing. The wages will be twenty-five each month. For everyone, no exceptions."

He glanced at John when he said it, indicating that, although he had no control over what other ranches did, there would be no discrimination on the Bar-U.

"We have some builders coming in soon, men. We all need good shelter for the cold months. The building crew will have us properly housed just as soon as possible. Now, go get that dinner."

After dinner John and Bill were walking together towards the unfinished cabin with their bedrolls over their shoulders. Fred called out to them, "Hold up there, fellas."

As they came close enough to speak comfortably Fred said, "John, I'd like to put you in charge of caring for the horses. There's nigh onto a hundred head. I'm told that even though the Blackfoot have hundreds of their own secreted back in those mountain valleys, that don't mean they won't make a try at ours. Seems they always have room for a few more head. I'd like you to choose one man to work with you. Perhaps Bill would want to do that."

"I'm more of a cattleman, Mr. Stimson," Bill responded. "But I know Al Deeves is a good horseman. You might ask him."

Stimson looked at John, passing the decision on to him.

"It's your call, John. You talk with Al. If the two of you can work together comfortably, that's fine with me. The decision is yours."

The manager of the North West Cattle Company walked away, indicating the pattern that was to follow. Men were to be given jobs and responsibility. No one was going to be looking over their shoulder as they faced those responsibilities. They were assigned a trust position. The rest was up to them.

John couldn't help reflecting back over the years, remembering when he rode away from the Shady Acres Farm all that time ago. He had been trusted with a nearly impossible task, given the reality of the war years and the slave situation. His freedom and a good horse and saddle were to be his reward. As unfamiliar as he had been with trust situations, he somehow knew that his dignity and character were at stake. He had been determined to prove up. And he did.

Now with responsibility for the Bar U horse herd, he would face the new responsibility with the same determination.

He sought out Al and pulled him aside where they could talk in confidence.

"Al, Mr. Stimson, he gave ol' John de job a car'n fer de remuda. Wants I should have 'nother man te work de horses along wit me. You be want'n to do dat?"

Al was in totally new territory with this question. Although he had balked a bit about joining a crew that included a black man, he had to face up to the fact that things hadn't been falling his way in Idaho. His need of a job had outshone his distaste at working with the unknown John. Now he was being asked to take second place to that same black man. To answer to him.

He admitted to himself, even if to no other, that John had more than proven himself over the hundreds of miles on the trail. That John was a good hand was no longer in question. But to be beholden to him. Even in as casual relationships as existed in the typical ranch job, well, that might be a stretch. But he did prefer horses over cattle. That couldn't be denied.

He knew his long pause was an indication of hard held beliefs, clearly obvious to John, and he was feeling some embarrassment. Finally, even without having made a firm decision, he heard himself saying, "Why shor, John, I'll work the horse herd with you."

It was his impetuous nature that had gotten him into trouble down in Idaho. He hoped that same nature would lead to a better outcome on the Bar U.

CHAPTER 4

For the first few days the horses showed no signs of wandering. The graze was good and the creek water plentiful. John and Al kept the animals close enough to the ranch headquarters to make roping out the day's workhorses an easier task. This was done in the evening, with Al doing most of the roping as each man called out his animal of choice. John hadn't completely given up on ever becoming a roper, but he was close to his last attempt. His many failures were the stuff of campfire humor as John himself told the stories.

The men tethered their chosen rides for the next day all around the small house.

The plan was to build a set of corrals before the winter temperatures turned the ground to stone, making it nearly impossible to dig a fence post hole. But until that was accomplished, there would be continual need for herding.

John and Al put in four easy, sun filled days riding wide around the herd, learning the country, watching for trouble and content when they found none. They carried their carbines in saddle boots so they would be prepared in the event of a visit from a grizzly, a prairie wolf, or, more likely more than one, since wolves were known to travel and hunt in their family groups. The biggest threat they saw was a small pack of coyotes skulking on the wide margins of the herd. They were really no threat. A coyote, with the help of his brothers could bring down a calf or a foal. But an adult horse was under no risk.

The task of herding horses was easily accomplished but was easing towards boredom after the first couple of days.

On the early evening of the fourth day, as the men were squeezing into the single log structure available to them, the wind stirred up. The building crew hadn't arrived and there was no shelter worthy of being called a refuge from a prairie storm. The men didn't know yet how to gauge the threat showing in these northern clouds, and the darkening sky, but even to unfamiliar eyes the evening looked ominous.

Although the ranch was still named formally as the North West Cattle Company, the crew had quickly adopted the Bar U as an easier title. Neither name meant much on the range as the cattle still carried their brands from Idaho. The chosen Bar U range was in naturally windy territory, just as most of the eastern edge of Rocky Mountain country was windy. From Colorado, north to Alberta, no one was surprised when a tie-down was needed to hold their Stetson in place. Flapping coat tails and filled eyes were taken as just a normal part of the job.

John remembered, with good humor, the Wyoming rancher that had hung a logging chain from a fence rail, as a wind gauge. But even with the familiarity of windy country, there was a menacing feel to the evening, as the men were spreading their blankets on the dirt floor. Wind streamers forcing their way through the unglazed window openings fluttered the kerosene lanterns.

A light howl preceded a change in the wind's direction, as it swung from west to northwest.

Several men walked outside to glance at the sky. The stars that had brightened the heavens an hour before were gone. In their place were high elevation streamers of wind-driven clouds, seen only as a contrast in color against the blacked sky. And the temperature was dropping. Clearly, noticeably dropping.

John pulled his jacket and hat on and walked out to the horses. Few of the animals were grazing. Most were standing, tail to the wind, with their heads held high and their ears straight up. There was no sign of the animals drifting but, knowing a wandering search for shelter could start at any time, John was concerned. After a half hour of walking and looking and listening, he went back to his blankets, determined to rise later, to check again.

The night herder with the cattle rode up to the shack after most of the men were asleep. Fred Stimson, the only man in the group with both a financial and managerial interest in the herd, was awake and watching the sky. He had staked out a position behind a short, protruding log wall where he was sheltered from the wind as well as he could be at the unfinished building. He saw the night herder approaching. Stepping out to where he could wave him over, he quietly waited for the man's report.

Not wishing to disturb the sleepers' rest time, Cliff Barrows spoke just above a whisper, saying, "I'm not familiar with this country Mr. Stimson, but if'n we was to be in Montana or Wyoming on a night like this

44

I'd be expecting cold and wind, probably snow. And drifting cattle. We could maybe hold them and maybe not. Most probably not. A longhorn brute, or even one of these crosses, with her tail to the wind is a determined creature. We have maybe an hour or two before we'll know the full of what's coming down on us, but if this was my herd, I'd have more riders out.

"That's your decision, boss. I'll ride back to the cattle and leave that thought with you."

"Thank you, Cliff. You can tell I'm worried some, else I'd be in my blankets. The country's new to me too. I take your warning. I'll keep my eyes peeled. But I'll let the men rest as long as possible."

Cliff lifted his hand in acceptance of that decision and rode back out to the herd.

Then the snow began to fall. Lightly at first, but drifting sideways, ahead of the northwest wind. The wind was lulled for a half hour while the snow fall became heavier, blanketing the entire country in white and bringing a hush across the land. A couple of men, sensing the new quiet, rose from their beds and stepped to the window cut-outs. Everything in sight was covered in white. Even as they watched, the wind picked back up. The snow already on

45

the ground, as light as feathers, began drifting across the land. The still falling snow was again driven sideways before the wind.

Fred Stimson was still holding down his chosen observation post behind the shelter of the log corner, although his feet were now cold, and he could sense the night's chill seeping through his warmest clothing. He didn't need years of experience in the country to know the snow was falling heavier by the minute, and the wind was beginning to howl its way into a true blizzard. Still, he hesitated in indecision.

Bill Moodie pulled his boots on when John rose from his bed. The two men walked outside, John to look to his horses, Bill to saddle his staked-out horse and ride out to help Cliff. Fred Stimson watched the two men as they went about caring for the Bar U animals, thankful that such experienced men existed and that they had chosen to throw their lot in with the North West Cattle Company.

Stimson waited another half hour before he admitted to himself that he was witnessing an early winter; a, no doubt about it, full out prairie storm. Finally, knowing that most of the men were already awake and wondering, he called them out.

"Men, we've got a real one blowing down

46

on us. I hate to call you out, but the two men out there now won't be able to hold those animals. I'd appreciate if you could ride to the south, get in front of the herd and try to keep them on Bar U range. I don't want a man hurt or certainly not killed, so you take care for yourselves. There's no telling what one of these frightened and determined wide-horned beasts might do. Stick together as much as possible. Ride in pairs at the very least."

Slowly and somewhat reluctantly, the men pulled on their boots and stood to their feet. They had warm coats, but were they warm enough for a night like this? Typical cowboys, mostly living for the present day and happy to let tomorrow wait for a new sunrise, they would not be thought of as planning, or forward-thinking men. Few had thought to purchase winter gloves or mitts, thinking there was time enough to do that on their next trip to The Crossing, although they had their big kerchiefs and three or four had woolen scarves.

Knowing what they were facing simply by listening, as the wind howled around the log structure and seeped through the window openings, each man, using kerchiefs or scarves or whatever was at hand, tied their Stetsons down. With coats buttoned to the throat and what gloves they had, pulled on, they went to their horses.

John, seeing that the horse herd was taking the storm more or less in stride, rode past the house, where Fred Stimson was still standing, studying the sky.

"De horses, dey be stay'n pretty good, I'm tink'n, Boss. I'm go help wit de cows, should dat be a'right wit you."

"Yes. Yes, of course, John. And I'll be here to keep an eye on the horses. For a while, at least."

The sky continued to darken until there was no sign of a shadow or reflection anywhere a man might look. The snow was falling steadily, building up thickly where the wind was unable to reach, and piling up in great drifts where that same wind dropped it, after coming against the slightest obstruction. A shrub or even a tuft of grass was enough to create an opportunity for a drift to form. Once a few flakes of snow stopped in one spot, others piled on, and then more and more. Before long what had begun as a small gathering at the slightest obstruction had become a drift, able to block horses or cattle from their chosen route.

The wind was now howling from almost due north. The cattle were heading almost due south. Although every man was game and every ridden horse was putting forth as much effort as conditions would allow, there was no holding the herd. Nor was there any chance of keeping it together. It split around bushes, around snow drifts, and around small rises in the prairie itself. Only rarely did the groupings come back together. Within minutes it was no longer a single herd, but many smaller herds, and then, even more bunches, sometimes only in twos or threes. The men were exhausting their mounts and themselves, as they did their best to bunch the determined animals again. But in the total blackness, with wind battering at their faces and snow getting into every slightest opening of their clothing and into their unprotected, squinting eyes, the men were losing track of their fellow riders, as well as the bulk of the herd.

Men that set their mounts to following and trying to turn ten or twelve cows, soon found themselves with only three or four animals within sight as the rest moved off thoughtlessly, in some other direction. Men who followed the breaking away group became separated from their riding partners with little hope of finding them again. It was a hopeless situation, and every man knew it.

Still, they worked. And still the horses

49

gave more than their all, until there was no more to give. A few men were forced to admit defeat when their horses simply stopped, turned their faces away from the wind and stood rigid, thoroughly chilled, refusing to obey either spur or rein. As the freezing and frightened cattle disappeared into the gloom of the night, the men finally, one by one, making their own decisions, turned back into the wind and the cabin, hoping against all odds that they had their directions right. To get lost on a night like this would mean hours of hunched shoulders and frozen feet and fingers and, at the extreme, could lead to death on the prairie grass. Three men, whose horses refused to carry them back north, dismounted and walked, tugging their horses by the reins.

Slowly they gathered back at the cabin. Fred Stimson had a fire burning in the center of the cabin floor. It would provide at least a little warmth on this cold sleepless night. He had secured a blanket over each of the window openings. It wasn't much but it was, at least, something to block the terrible wind. He had hung two lit lanterns on the south corners of the cabin, hoping the men would see them through the storm and could beacon back on them in their return ride. He understood full well that men and animals were now at the mercy of the storm, and their own strength and resources. He prayed the men would understand and turn back.

Within a half hour all but three men were accounted for. Fred stood at the doorway, watching in vain for movement. The blowing snow was blocking out all but the merest glimpse of the land. Finally, one man, walking and leading his horse came into view. Fred ran out and took the horse from the rider. Bending low to the man's ear he hollered, "Fire inside. Go get yourself in there. I'll care for the horse."

It was another full hour before a second rider hove into sight. The man was also walking. He nearly collapsed as Fred ran to pull him in. He could barely talk through nearly frozen lips and chin, but he managed to say, "Lost. Lost. Thank God for those lanterns."

"Fire inside. Get yourself in there. Leave the horse to me."

The man dropped the reins and staggered to the cabin.

Although Fred had said he would care for the horse, he could do nothing but unsaddle the animal and turn it loose. There had been no time to put up any hay at the home place, although before the herd had arrived, the two riders on the payroll had put up a couple of tons, storing it beside an old shack someone had built a few miles away, and abandoned long ago. What feed the horses managed would be found beneath the snow they, themselves scraped away.

Now, only John was unaccounted for. The men, unable to hide their concern, discussed the possibilities.

"Might have made it to the Crossing."

"Could be at the shack out west where we stacked that hay."

"Folks named Quirk, or some such, got a shack and a few head on grass, back towards the Crossing. He'd be fine if he could make it there."

"Could be holed up in a treed hollow."

"Could be almost anywhere."

What no one wanted to admit is that John could just as easily be in serious trouble. Possibly even dead, with his body covered under drifting snow.

The men had no choice but to hover around the cabin for the next three days while the land gave way to the total domination of the storm. Nothing, human nor animal, could compete with the wind or the cold or the ever-deepening snow. They were long days with little to do beyond gathering up the few horses that hadn't wandered too far in their attempt to find wind-cleared graze that would sustain life. The men's days alternated between troubling silence, talk, worry and waiting.

On the fourth morning, the wind died down to its normal, drifting breeze, the snow stopped falling when the clouds lightened and then drifted away. The late fall sun broke through onto a world of dazzling white.

The horses had found barely enough graze to keep them alive. Their strength was depleted, and they were reluctant to be saddled or put to work. But the experienced riding crew each selected the most likely animal for the long search, saddled up and headed south, hoping to find the Bar U herd. Or at least, most of it.

Fred Stimson sent the men out in pairs with warning to watch out for each other and not get separated. For safety, the men tied bedrolls behind their saddles and took a bit of food with them. Each man replenished his supply of matches.

"There's no telling if the storm is truly over or if it's just resting, readying itself for another blow."

Fred asked Bill Moodie to pair him off. He assigned positions from the foothills to the Fort Macleod Trail to the other pairs of men. They would have miles between them and could easily miss something, but it was the best they could do with the number of men available. He chose the most easterly position for himself. He would ride first to the Crossing to gather whatever news might be available, and then move south, following the Macleod Trail, if it was identifiable beneath the snow.

There was little news at the Crossing, but the two Bar U riders did manage to get a hot meal and a cup of coffee at the Smith and French establishment. Smith was somewhat cavalier about the whole matter. He had seen storms before. Their small, combination store, eating-house and hotel, was well buttoned down and able to withstand whatever the country threw its way.

"Ain't seen hide nor hair of man nor beast since the storm hit. Cept'n those what belong here, is what I mean to say. Anyway, with the snow rid 'n the wind down from the north it's doubtful that any Bar U stuff would wander crossways to it and come ta visit French and me. No, you'd best be rid'n south. Way that wind was blow'n you might have to ride some ways to catch up to whatever animals ain't froze and lyin' under a drift somewhere."

As Fred and Bill were riding away Bill

looked over at his riding partner and boss and said, "Encouraging fella."

Fred hunched his shoulders beneath his heavy coat and grinned as he glanced back towards Bill.

"Not much tenderness or love for his fellow man in either Smith or French, but that don't make him wrong. Anyway, it ain't likely any soft handed store clerk could hold out in this new land. A new land needs fellas like Smith and French. Being the first and showing the way is not for the weak-willed, or the faint of heart. Those types will be along soon enough to pick up the pieces left lying around by their betters."

"We knew it was well-nigh impossible we'd find any Bar U stock over this way. But we had to find out, and check, too, for any news."

Bill hesitated before completing his boss' thought for him.

"Be nice to hear something of John though."

Fred chose not to respond. Instead, he said, "We'll swing back west some and south. The Quirks have settled somewhere in this area. Met them just the once but never been to their place. Good folks. Up from Montana. Mrs. Quirk is the first white woman to take up residence in the area. A bit strange, they are. Like to stay to themselves. But good folks just the same. If John rode in from the night, they would sure enough welcome him in."

There had been no sign of John Ware at the Quirks' place. But the good-natured John Quirk had left Fred and Bill with a further challenge.

"I had three hundred head branded with a Q, before the storm. Not a single one in sight today. I expect someone will find them by 'n by and push them this way. You might keep an eye open."

As they were riding away Bill, who was much more talkative than Fred, said, "Didn't appear to be much concerned about those three hundred head."

Fred had a simple explanation. "Some folks figure it's just one of two ways. They'll be found, or they won't. Not much else to it."

It wasn't until Fred flagged down the Calgary bound stage that was fighting its way northward, breaking a trail through the drifts, that any positive information was received. In truth, it was a mixture of positive and, possibly, negative.

Fred explained their presence on the trail. The driver listened and then responded, "You'll find nothing along this way for many a mile to the south. Your stuff must be off to the west somewhere. The only sign we saw was a good lot of miles further along to the south. Less snow, a bit of graze poking its heads out of the snow down that way. Saw a bunch of cattle off to the west of the trail. Too far to the west to get much detail. Appeared to be just the one rider among them. All I saw anyway. Too far away to make out who it might be. And that's some hours ago. Got no other news that might help you."

Fred already had his horse in motion when he hollered, "Thanks. We'll check it out."

Fred was worried and showing his concern. Bill kept his thoughts to himself, waiting for the boss to lead the way in his thinking. It took some time but finally Fred said, "The only man we're missing is John and there's no way he could be that far south. So, who could the rider be? You don't suppose it's possible some maverick rider is pushing a bunch, hoping to make it to the border before anyone catches up with him?"

Bill had no response.

CHAPTER 5

By the time the two searchers came in sight of the cattle, they could see, even from the distance, that the animals had quit their southward movement and were eagerly pulling at the generous portion of grass that was protruding through the now settled snow. As the need to say something was building up in Bill, Fred was remaining silent, with his eyes firmly glued on the south-west horizon. Finally, with an expression of defeat, he said, "Glare off the snow's so bad a man can't see nothing at all. Could go blind out here."

"Heard about it. Years ago." answered Bill. "Heard about it, but never seen it or experienced it till I got to Montana some while back. Knew a fella that blinded himself to where he had to lay low till spring. Even then he had trouble with his eyes. Bad business, that. I've been squinting tight for most of an hour now. Helps some. Still can't make out any rider. This bunch might have pulled themselves together after the storm let up, rider or no."

The men rode in silence for a while before Bill's thoughts again burst from his lips.

"You take horses, now, they're like the deer or elk or other wild beasts. They can make out for the full of a winter, taking what moisture they need from the snow in the stead of water, and scratching the snow away to get to the grass below. But cow critters, they'd fail if'n they were held off water for long. Get by with the snow they pull into their mouths along with the graze for a short while. Keep them alive maybe, but by 'n by they're going to be wandering again, looking for water."

Fred acknowledged the truth of this with a nod of his head that Bill couldn't have seen, with his eyes squinted almost tight shut.

A slow half hour of riding, the horses making their way carefully through the knee-deep snow, as the footing was questionable at best, brought them close to a small hollow in a cluster of prairie brush; willows and such. A slow drift of smoke was rising through the bare branches. No man or men were in sight, but Fred was being cautious.

"Those cows didn't set that fire to going.

There's at least one man down in that hollow. If we're dealing with a rustler, Bill, that could be a branding fire."

Bill, who had much more experience with cattle, snow and cowboys, came close to chuckling but he managed to tamp it down, simply saying, "Ain't likely. Just the one man, or even two. Not about to go to blotting brands out on this flat, snow-covered range. My guess is that it's a fire to keep a body from dropping dead with cold."

Agree or not, Fred opened his eyes wide, risking snow blindness again and nudged his horse to a bit more speed, prepared to crash through the brush, shooting as he rode, if that proved to be necessary. Easterner he may be, and unfamiliar with the idiosyncrasies and habits of the west, but these were his cattle and he planned to have them back.

The only sounds to break the morning's stillness were the swishing of the horse's feet as he stepped through the snow, and a slight saddle creak as Fred leaned forward, intent on his quarry.

Bill thought to caution his boss, warning that they hadn't seen the brands on the animals yet. These might not be Bar U cattle. In any case, the North West Cattle Company herd hadn't been re-branded yet.

They still carried the four brands of the different Idaho ranches they had been purchased from. The blacksmith-built Bar U branding iron had never been used.

But Fred had made up his mind. These were his cattle. Who else could they possibly belong to? There were few ranches yet on this grass, and none as large as the numbers of these grazing animals suggested. He would check the brands later. With all of that in mind and convinced that whoever was at the fire was up to nothing good, he let out a roar and charged his horse into the brush. Bill looked on in some dismay. Clearly, it was far too late to hope Fred would listen to any warning.

Bill hadn't reached under his heavy coat for his pistol, doubting it would be needed, but Fred crashed into the little hollow, prepared to fight and shoot if challenged. Fortunately, the man by the fire had chosen a well sheltered spot that Fred couldn't ride directly into. It was fortunate also, that the man was of a cool nature. He had obviously heard Fred crashing through the brush. Bill, following close behind his boss, but still unable to see what Fred was up to, was pleased when no gun battle erupted on the snow-covered Alberta plains that morning.

In place of a conflict and the sting and

stink of burnt powder, or branded and burnt hair, either one, Fred and Bill were greeted with, "Morn'n, Boss. Bill. If'n you wished, you could come get yourselves warm by de fire. Got a bit a deer meat left too, if'n you should be hungry."

Fred pulled his horse to a snow scattering stop and squinted into the sun glazed, snow covered camp.

"John? Is that you, John?"

"Dat shore enough be ol' John, Boss. Jes' me, no one else be here."

"My god, man. We'd about given up on you. Thought we'd maybe find you in the spring after the snow went off."

"Come mighty near be'n how it was, Boss. Wasn't fer dis couple a acres a brush ol' John jest could a been sing'n wit de angels come dis time. I spects de good lawd, he know ol' John, he cain't sing so good an lef me wit de cows fer dis time. Maybe 'nother time he let me join de choir."

Bill tied his horse to a willow bush and walked to the fire. He and John shook hands while Bill said, "John, you old rascal. You not only have a fire to welcome visitors, but you've got a haunch of venison to show your hospitality. It's good to see you alive and with some cattle under your control."

"Ain't really under control, Bill. Dey doi'n

jest what dey wants de do fo' de last days. Dey be gather'n demselves together last day er two. Mos' all de herd might be to dis place."

"All ol' John able ta do was follow along. Horse, he be pretty much played out. Me too, come ta dat. Cold. Almighty cold, dat wind. Den de wind drop and I see dis little place. See de deer be struggle through de snow, nearly dead from de struggle. I grab his horns and pull de knife. Pretty soon I's got de fire goi'n an de steak a-cook'n."

Fred had secured his horse by this time and walked to the fire. He and John shook in silence, Fred's eyes showing his relief at finding this man alive and apparently well.

Fred finally looked around him at the sparseness of the camp. He saw nothing more than a hollowed-out shelter where John had scooped the snow from under the gathered brush, placing his fire at the mouth of the snow cave, for reflected warmth. He found himself wondering how this former slave from the warm south lands had figured out that a snow cave, although falling a sight short of a luxury hotel room, could keep a man alive.

His mind was going over the fierceness of the storm and the four days that had passed since it started. Any man looking on would clearly see that it was close to a miracle that the country had left anyone alive.

"I purely don't know how you survived, John. But I'm almighty glad you did. We've been out for most of the day and my feet are feeling like they just might snap off, they're so cold. My fingers too. And I suspect my ears, and perhaps my nose are all edging towards frost bite."

Bill added his thought to Fred's, "Did you have other fires, John, or how did you survive?"

"Jes dis one fire. Was shore enough cold. Still cold. I never used dose tight rid'n boots you fellas be wear'n. Not comfortable fo' my big feet. Dee's here boots a mine be big and loose. Be better, but my feet, still dey gett'n cold. Hands, I kep' in my pockets. Horse, he jes' be follow'n de cows. He don need ol' John fer dat. I kep' de hands in de pockets and jes' ride along. He stop when de cattle go to graz'n on dat long grass out der. Shore lak to be somewhere's else tho, lak maybe de warm bed, 'n a bunk house."

Fred said, "Let's cook up a bit of that venison, like you suggested, John, then we'll head for Fort Macleod. It can't be too far off. The cattle aren't going anywhere now that they have some graze."

■ ■ ■ ■

After a long night's sleep in warm beds in Kamoose Taylor's Fort Macleod Hotel the three Bar-U men were ready to make decisions and face up to the demands of cattle raising in a very demanding country. But then, all cattle country can be demanding in one way or another. Discussing the matter over breakfast, Fred had little to say. The born and raised eastern Canadian had no experience with the land to the south. But wishing to be more knowledgeable, he asked questions of Bill and John and listened carefully to the answers.

Both men had trailed cattle all the way from Texas to Montana, at different times, stopping off at frontier cattle centers like Dodge City and Cheyenne, and many smaller rest stops along the way.

It was not many years earlier that John would have been whipped for entering into a conversation between white men. But those days were now past, at least on the western frontier. Perhaps his freedom would be more constrained in the big cities, but what was happening there was of no interest to John. His life was one of horses and cattle, ranching and big country.

Fred made it plain that John's experience and knowledge would be valuable in the decisions made by the North West Cattle Company manager.

"Well, Boss. I's gues'n der's trouble enough no matter where a fella might be get'n to in dis here ol' world. Sure, be warmer down to Fort Worth, but den de cows, dey be walk'n long way to de water. An de grass be no such as dis be here. Even one cow be need'n two, three acres a land, maybe more, ta git enough ta eat. And de cowboys, dey be rid'n long way ta gather up de cattle an' brand de calves. Lots a brush an rough country fer to hide de critters. Maybe-so dis not be sech a bad country."

Bill entered the conversation with, "John's right, Fred. On some drives we went days without water. Poor critters frantic with thirst and the sun beating down on their hides until they couldn't even sweat for lack of water. And don't ever fool yourself, anywhere north of Texas can be cold and snowy. You want to see cold and snow and wind, you spend a winter in Wyoming. Great country and beautiful as all get out, with the mountains off to the west, but no bargain to live in or raise beef in.

"No, I expect this last storm, although a real humdinger, wasn't typical of the country. It might be an indication though, that it would be wise to build some haystacks for future winters, and a fence or two."

The conversation went on for some time, with Fred listening and considering, until he finally said, "Fellas, we're going to leave the cattle where they are. They're not going to wander away from that feed. What we're going to do, is, we're going to ride back to the ranch and detail off a crew to spend the winter down here. I'll go to the trading post and order up tents and supplies before we leave.

"We'll outfit the crew as best as the local supplies will allow. There's work enough back at the ranch so we'll have to keep a few men there. We didn't take time to count those animals, but I expect it's less than the entire herd. There'll be more Bar U's wandering to the west. The boys can ride out for a look see. We'll have losses, but perhaps fewer than I feared.

"Now, let's get over to the trading post. I'll purchase for the ranch. You boys may want to gear up with warmer clothing, mitts and a winter hat with ear flaps. It's not even Christmas yet so I expect we've got some winter ahead of us."

Fred sent Bill and John off to the west on

their return to the ranch headquarters, looking for both cattle and riders who might still be out or who had ridden out again. He, himself would ride to the Crossing to spread his news of the herd, and of John's survival, and pick up any news that may have come in from others.

...

CHAPTER 6

The men that volunteered to spend the
winter in the tent camp on the south range
were given a temporary increase in pay in
recognition of the expected hardships and
extra work. In addition, Fred commissioned
Jerry Potts to find a cook for the south crew.
He came back with a Blackfoot woman who
had cooked for the whisky traders' trading
post at Fort Whoop up, and, on occasion,
for Kamoose Taylor at his Fort Macleod
Hotel.

   She had let the whisky traders know in
the clearest language that she was cook only.
Any misunderstanding on that point would
bring on unwelcome results, for the traders.
She had mastered only a little English, but
she emphasized her point, making it clear
while brandishing a ten-inch skinning knife.

   The cook was introduced by Jerry, only as
Kanti. She took it as personal pride that no
white man knew her full Blackfoot name. A

small thing perhaps, but important to Kanti. Her personal dignity was about the last thing remaining from her once grand, but now devastated tribe.

Looking over the temporary cattle camp, and the men who were to winter there, while remaining seated on her horse, she simply nodded to Jerry and turned her horse back towards Macleod. Jerry said, "Boys, you got you a cook. But she's just the cook. Don't you be misunderstanding that. She still carries the knife she skinned buffalo with. She'd have no trouble at all in skinning a cowboy. You treat her right. Help her all you can. Drag in some wood. Keep the fire going. Bring in some meat, time to time. Ain't no other cook that's going to show up way out here.

"Now, fellas, I'll ride back to town with her, put together a load of camp supplies and bring her back out tomorrow. It would help if you could clear the snow from a goodly sized camp area and form up a fire ring. Find some flat rocks for the holding of pots and such."

With no further words Jerry turned and followed Kanti back to the Fort.

West of the headquarters ranch, Bill and John scoured the foothills for cattle or cattle tracks. They managed to drive about one hundred head of half-starved animals out of the rocks and light forest skirting the edge of the Rockies themselves. They saw no other sign of riders. Judging by tracks, no horses had wandered this far. Elk, on the other hand were plentiful. So were the wolves that fed on them.

The elk were wily and tough to bring down, unwilling as they were to be winter feed for their fiercest enemy. It was unlikely that a single wolf would find success in a go-around with an adult elk, who fought predators off with hooves and horns. But the wolf didn't hunt alone. The wolf was a pack animal, presenting a risk to his quarry from many directions at once. The rancher's concern was that the wolf would soon discover that beef animals had no real instinct for self-defense, now that the true longhorn was either bred out of them or that the longhorn crosses had been replaced with heavier, slower Eastern or European breeds. And, of course, the calves were totally defenseless to a hungry and determined predator.

John and Bill drove their small gather east, towards the rough cabin where the hay had been stacked. When they arrived, they discovered that the elk were there before

71

them. A considerable amount of hay was scattered on top of the snow, with some trampled into the ground, underfoot. With much shouting and arm waving as they rode their horses among the elk, plus a few shots from saddle guns, they managed to drive the elk off.

They ran off, but they didn't go far. Bill figured it would take constant diligence if the ranch was going to save any hay at all for the cattle, which was the single reason the Bar U existed at all.

The starving cattle settled in around the shack, eagerly making up for the grazing they had missed during the storm. Sitting their horses, side by side, as they watched the cattle eat, Bill said, "We got us a problem here, John. These cows got to be driven to join up with the big bunch over to the main camp. But if we both leave here the elk will destroy all the work the boys did in putting up this feed."

John replied, "How it be, I drive dis bunch back to de camp. You stay here. Keep de elk off'n de cut grass. You kin light de fire an' cook yo'self up a nice steak, should it be you happen to shoot one of dem elk. I be back maybe in two, three days. Bring de wagon. Maybe-so we's take dis grass to de main camp."

Bill thought of that for a minute, grinned and looked at his riding partner.

"I don't know about that, John. It seems to me you're setting yourself up to have all the fun. I've got to keep a fire going and skin out an elk, at least a haunch, cooking up my own food, whilst all you've got to do is guide a hundred starving and freezing beef critters over twenty miles of frozen and snow-covered ground, with no feed or water for them. Hardly anything to it at all. Should hire kids for simple tasks like that."

John, fully aware that Bill was offering to reverse the responsibilities, simply said, "Well, dey not be so starv'n now dey been chew'n on dat cut grass. I's tink maybe-so I get wood fer de fire. You shoot de elk. Ol' John not so good wit de gun as you be. I try one a dem steaks you's talk'n bout before I take'n de cows out a here."

Wordlessly, Bill turned his horse and reached for the .44-40 saddle gun. John went on foot to the nearby bush hoping to drag in some wood that wasn't frozen into the ground. Within a couple of hours, one of the numerous elk that had been enjoying the easily accessible hay had been shot and butchered. The odor of cooking steaks that were hung over the coals on the edge of the fire took over the camp site.

While Bill was busy demonstrating his shooting and butchering skills, John had scrounged up a supply of wood that should hold Bill in some comfort for a full day or more.

"Dat be a good steak. Bill. Maybe-so you not go hungry before Ol' John get back wit de wagon."

"Maybe-so you're right, John. Now, that's a long trail for just one man to guide these cattle through. I know you'll do everything possible, but if a few drop off along the way don't worry about them. We'll pick them up on the next trip. I'm hoping you'll take care of yourself."

"I be alright. Git dis little bunch back to home and come wit de wagon fer de hay. Maybe-so be back in two days."

"More like three, John."

The two cowboys worked together to push the animals off the hay and get them gathered into a bunch. Bill stayed with John until the gather covered its first mile, pushing a path through the deep snow. The cattle would tire quickly with that kind of walking, but John had no intention of allowing them to slow down or stop until he reached the Bar U headquarters. Through the afternoon and into the dark of night the little cavalcade kept moving, not quickly, but moving.

It was mid-morning the next day when the smoke from the cook fire pierced a grey beacon into the air, pointing the direction to the main camp.

With his horse and himself both about done in, and the cattle staggering with fatigue, John lifted his carbine and fired three quick shots into the air. As he had hoped, he soon saw several mounted cowboys heading his way. Wordlessly, knowing exactly what was needed, the men pulled between John and the herd, taking over the drive. John, weary beyond description himself, knew his horse was in even worse shape. He dismounted, pulled the reins over the horse's head and set out afoot, allowing the animal to complete the homeward walk without bearing John's considerable weight.

As he had promised Bill, John was up and preparing for the wagon trip back to the hay pile early the following morning. The camp owned just the one flat-deck wagon and a single yoke of oxen for the pulling of it. John had little experience with oxen and was making a hard job of their harnessing. Cliff Barrows came to his rescue. With John as an eager and apt learner, the job was soon done.

"You going to be alright with that by

yourself from here on, John?"

"You is a good teacher, Cliff. I be alright."

As was common, John caught and saddled a fresh horse for the return trip to the foothills shack. He would ride beside the oxen, guiding and encouraging them along the way.

A few days later, after several trips with the wagon, the hay was safely stacked at the main camp. The men protected it from the always hungry beef animals with a roughly put together fence of dead falls and cut branches. It was nowhere near enough hay, but with the grazing boosted by the periodic feeding of the precious stacked grass, the ranch hoped to bring most of the main camp animals through the winter.

A couple of the riders, who had witnessed the miracle of chinook winds in other parts of the eastern slope of the Rockies, kept looking hopefully to the west. The saving of the herd might very well depend on those warming winds. But there was no telling when that beautiful tell-tale chinook arch would form over the mountains, announcing a major change in the weather.

Some chinooks lasted barely a few hours. Others lasted several days, melting the snow down and exposing the grass beneath. With one eye to the western horizon, the men worked and watched and hoped.

With the constant herding, feeding and chopping of ice from the small river's edge, the crew did manage to bring most through the winter. The cows, now heavy with calf, were more and more reluctant to walk miles, or scramble for the remaining native grasses. Even the grass that the occasional chinook had exposed was eaten down for a good distance from the ranch headquarters. The men were grazing the animals further and further away, putting them, in turn, further from the water source.

The coming of spring seemed to linger, but when the last of the snow finally melted off the grazing grounds, the hard-working men heaved a great sigh of relief.

CHAPTER 7

Fred Stimson rode to the Crossing hoping to find George Emerson. Emerson was quickly expanding his reputation as pioneer rancher and cattleman, while adding town enthusiast and builder to those titles. George, with his old partner Tom Lynch had trailed the first herds into the area. They had set up their ranch on the wide grasslands off to the west, in foothills country. The same general area Fred himself had chosen for the North West Cattle Company. Tom was running the ranch while George pursued his other multiple interests.

Emerson heard his name singled out in a question posed to Smith in Stimson's booming voice.

"Morn'n, Smith. You seen anything of Emerson lately? Like to get ahold of him. Got a thing or two to talk over."

Smith simply pointed his thumb over his shoulder, towards the small area of his establishment that he called his saloon. What it was, in fact, was a poor imitation of a western saloon, along with a couple of tables for the serving of food. Asking no further questions, Stimson nodded his thanks and turned to the doorway that was draped with a tanned elk hide that was still wearing the hair. Pushing the curtain aside, Fred boomed out, "George, I been looking all over town for you and here you sit, doing nothing at all that matters, just drinking Smith and French out of coffee."

George slowly laid his coffee mug on the table, leaned back in his chair, turned towards the voice and said, "Well. Fred. Ain't but the two places to look here at the Crossing. Smith's place or the outhouse. Mind you, you come here in ten years that ain't going to be the case. This here is an up-and-coming metropolis. Why, I was just thinking . . ."

"Ya, ya. I know all that. Heard you expound on it a time or two. But that's then. This here I need to talk to you about is now. The wind you're expecting to blow then ain't gonna turn no windmills now."

"Well, since there ain't a single windmill in the whole country, what you say is probably true. Mind, a windmill or two just could be the answer to our dry summers.

Hard to tell what this land would grow, should it have water poured on it from time to time. Or how well our beef would grow if they always had water close to hand."

"You're correct again, George, but right at this very time we have a situation. We've got cattle spread over more square miles than I ever knew existed and we got to gather them up. We've got Cochrane animals from way up along the Bow, and we've got brands I never seen nor heard about before, from way down around Macleod, all mixed together. We need to get them sorted out and brought home. And we sure don't need what's left of the Cochrane bunch eating our grass.

"There'll be calves that need branding and more calves coming along, time to time through the spring. They need to be where our own riders can care for them, keeping the coyotes away and watch'n over the birthing's. We've got to have a roundup."

George studied his friend with a knowing eye, understanding exactly what the visit was about, but he still asked the question.

"I suppose you've nailed the situation accurately enough but what has that got to do with me? I guess whatever needs there are with the Rocking P animals, ol' Tom Lynch is capable of taking care of. Good cattleman, Tom. I rest easy of a night knowing that Tom's looking after things."

Fred, picking up the semi-jesting nature of the conversation said, "Tom's a good man. On a trail drive or running a ranch, you couldn't want for better. No doubt of that. Maybe the best there is. But he's not the organizer you are. Tom and I together, along with Cochrane and some others, couldn't gather the ranchers together as well as you could. We need a roundup George, and it's you that has to call it."

French wandered in from somewhere in the labyrinth of the ramshackle 'stopping place' and said, "You boys hungry for lunch, or are you just going to sit there drinking up my coffee and making noise? Don't seem to be any way for Smith and myself to make a living, what with the likes of you two helping yourselves to the coffee pot."

Over lunch the two men planned the roundup. Fred would gather the local crew and find something that would pass as chuckwagons while George got the word out to the ranches, large and small, none of them over one year old. With that decided, George asked, "What's next for the North West Cattle Company, Fred?"

Fred, never tiring of talking about his cattle company and the wonderful country he was situated in, answered with some enthusiasm.

"I've got a crew of carpenters coming down from Calgary. And that was no easy thing to accomplish. They were supposed to be here in the fall, but the big storm put a stop to that. They've had no end of building business offered to them in Calgary this spring. I had to up the ante, dig into my pockets a bit deeper, just to drag them away from the big city. But we're going ahead with the bunkhouse and what I'm calling the main house, although I hope to build a more welcoming place come by and by. If the Allan brothers or any of their wealthy friends decide to visit, I'll want to be able to put them up in some comfort."

George interrupted Fred long enough to ask, "I suppose you have a good enough situation as manager and part owner of the brand but why don't you buy out the Allans? Go on your own?"

"Well, my friend. There are two good reasons for that. The first is that the Allans have no intention of selling. The second is that if they were to sell, I wouldn't have the ready funds to buy. In the meantime, they finance everything and pretty much leave me alone. And the little bit of funding I can call my own, beyond what is already in this

Alberta outfit, is safely invested back east.

"Anyway, as I was saying, before you posed a question you already knew the answer to, we're planning some outbuildings. We need a barn for the horses and an icehouse for the storing of meat and such. I've got the boys cutting and hauling spruce poles down from the hills, for a set of working corrals. Lots of other plans. Won't all get done this summer but by fall we'll at least need a bunkhouse and cookhouse to get the men out of the cold. I don't suppose the crew would stay with me for another winter like this last one. That was a tough go."

George, never having to leave the Crossing or the Smith and French establishment, exerted his considerable influence by sending out three riders with a message from him. The riders were to take the news to every rancher north of the Oldman River, as far north as the Bow. As many as they could locate anyway. Some of the smaller, hardscrabble outfits, mostly men who were looking to get away from a past that had left them broke and seeking solitude, had pushed their few animals deep into the forests and foothills. Those men would show themselves when they were ready, and not before.

"Don't you fellas be long in getting the word spread around. The boys are to meet up at Fort Macleod two weeks from today. They're to come geared up for a one-month push. Grub will be supplied. We'll cover the expenses with the sale of a few dogie calves. They need to bring extra horses. The days will be long. No one horse is about to see them through those long hours. Tell them if they're expecting calves to bring their branding irons with them."

Two days before the gathering of men were to meet up at the Fort, John, Bill Moodie and Ab Cotterell put the Bar U headquarters behind them as they headed south. Three other riders had accompanied Fred Stimson to the Crossing the day before to help with the purchasing and transporting of supplies for the Bar U crew, and to add to the foodstuffs put together by the three hired cooks. The other Bar U men remained behind to herd and care for the cattle and horses left on the home range. These men would have to show special care for the newborn calves. The coyotes seemed to be thicker on the ground than they were the year before. Perhaps feeding off the multitude of downed and winter killed stock had fed the predators into a good birthing year with more pups surviving than what was usual.

With the southbound riders busy the first couple of hours holding the remuda of loose horses, preventing them from splitting and heading off in different directions, there was little talk between them. But finally, the horses figured it out and settled down to a steady trot, under the watchful eyes of the three men.

Bill, never one to intrude into someone else's affairs, was studying Ab Cotterell, as that rider was working his mouth as if he were chewing on a stiff, cold piece of jerky. Clearly, the man had something on his mind. Ab, the ramrod on the drive from Idaho to the Bar U, as the first big herd was brought north, was regarded as a good cattleman and a knowing leader of men. Bill had no idea what was troubling his friend but chose to say nothing.

A few minutes later, Ab solved the mystery with a question.

"Either of you fellas know what the date is?"

John chose not to state his opinion, not being too sure himself. Nor caring overmuch. Bill chuckled and said, "Why shore, Ab. The fact that the snow is gone, and the country is greening up with new grass, with millions of wildflowers everywhere a man wishes to look, might all add up to the truth that this is May. Spring. And welcome it is, too."

"Ya well, I know enough to sort all of that out. What do you think? I don't know spring from fall? I meant: what year is it?"

Bill couldn't help himself. He burst into raucous laughter. John smiled a bit but again didn't say anything. As a slave, one year was about like another. It was only for the past decade or so that he had ever really been aware of the numbering of the years. He thought he knew the date, but he would remain out of the conversation, just the same.

Ab feigned deep hurt with a sad look at Bill.

"Should have fired you from the drive crew and sent you back south on the trip up from Idaho. Could'a and should'a done it. A man what will laugh at his riding pard ain't no man to ride the river with. Anyway, it's a simple question. Trouble is, I'm coming to think you don't know the answer either. Neither you nor John, either one."

Bill quieted his laughter and spoke to John. "What do you think, John? What year is it?"

"I ain't got no strong opinion on dat Boss. Nor hav'n no need ta know. Ol' John ain't about ta go nowhere. Jest rid'n dis here half broke horse, hop'n to git the scramble otta his head by de time we's git to de Fort. I 'spect we all gonna git der on de same year anyway."

Bill again directed his insight to Ab, saying, "There you go, my friend. It don't matter what year it is. You've got John's word and wisdom on that. But just supposing, with you chewing over the matter, it's going to keep you from doing your work, adding extra load on my shoulders, I'll set your mind at ease. It's the year of our Lord, eighteen hundred and eighty-three. May of that year to be exact."

"You sure of that? You ain't pulling my leg, are you?"

"Naw. I ain't mak'n no game of it. It's for sure eighteen eighty-three. That present a problem for you?"

"Well, my folks, down to home might be thinking it's a problem. I promised to write, let them know that I was still alive. And I did too. Once. I've been pretty busy since that time."

"When was that? When you wrote, I mean?"

"Why, I remember that plainly. It was

eighteen eighty. I remember because there was a lot of celebrating and hoopla about the new decade marking out the arrival of civilization. Some figured it that way anyway. That was down in a little town in Nebraska. Forgot its name. Might have blown away by now. Don't matter anyhow. Wasn't much to celebrate in that shack setup but we took it as an opportunity to have a drink and maybe-so dance with a lady, suppos'n one should be inclined that way."

Bill wasn't finished giving advice.

"You should oughta get you one of them picture photographs taken. Send it along with the letter."

Ab studied his friend as they rode along, before saying, "Why, that ain't no way a half bad idea."

Fred Stimson, sitting tall on his gelding on the outskirts of Fort Macleod, looked over the gathered riders. The local police commandant, James Hyer, studied the group as well. Both men were taking a quick count of the gathering. James stored the number in his mind and turned to his friend, saying, "I come to about forty-five riders there, Fred. That's a goodly crew but you've got a big territory to cover. I suspect you'll need every man, and you'll most likely still miss a few cows."

Fred nodded, silently agreeing with James' count. For some reason he couldn't quite put his fingers on, he felt an unfamiliar emotion at the sight of the gathering. For a transplanted city man, the emotion was unusual and unexpected. He had heard the tales around the evening fires of the great cattle drives. The rough comradery. The lifelong friendships that were born. The long days. The dust. The heat. The often-inedible grub. The fearsome risks from horns and hooves. The refusal to ride with men who had shown themselves to be less than trustworthy. The stampedes. The loss of a man along the way, buried in a lonely grave that no one would ever find again. The celebrations at the end of the trail.

Fred had neither seen nor experienced anything like that. The short drive with the original herd, from Fort Macleod to the ranch's chosen headquarters site held no comparison.

He slumped a bit in the saddle before responding to James.

"Take a good look, James. You'll never see the likes again. Oh, there'll be other round-ups. Lots of them. Bigger ones than this. But those men you see out there are the cream of the crop. The leaders. The builders. The first on the scene. There are men out on that grass whose names will be written down in Alberta history and studied a century from now. Every newly settled country needs men like that. Alberta pioneers, one and all.

"Why just look. There's George Emerson, he of the Rocking P brand. He's already established one of the first ranches on the Alberta grass and now he's set his mind to turning The Crossing into a real enough town. He'll be known one day as the father of The Crossing. Or whatever they name the new town. Then there's Tom Lynch. No better trail driver or cattleman ever lived. And beside him is John Quirk. John's wife is the first white woman to settle in the area. Good folks. Independent.

"Then there's Herb Miller," he said pointing. "To his right is Phil Weinard. There's Duncan Cameron. Ab Cotterell."

Looking carefully, he sorted them out. "There's Bill Moodie and Fred Ings. Frank Strong. Cattlemen all. Men fit to build a ranch. Or a nation.

"The strange thing is, James, most of those fellas, George Emerson, who has a tight grasp on history a-building, being the lone exception, have no understanding of what they've already done or what they're yet going to do. They don't hold much pride to themselves beyond their riding and herding abilities, and the hopes that they'll be known and remembered as a man to ride the river with, as they love to say. That they were good men and good pards. That each one is much bigger than that, they may never understand. But those following after, those who write, and study history will understand.

"Beside those men, but in some ways, above them, you'll see John Ware. The first man of color I ever worked with. The first in the territory so far as I know. First one I've ever seen anyway. The best man with horses on this range. Strong, stalwart, faithful. Never seems to tire and never seems to be unhappy. If he's got a weakness, it's that he has a bit of an itchy foot. It's going to be hard to hold him in one place. Always seems to be ready and willing to look over the fence at a new opportunity or adventure. I'm hoping to be able to keep him on the Bar U, but time will tell on that.

"Great men all. I feel it to be a privilege to ride beside such men."

CHAPTER 8

The roundup crew was split into three groups, each with their own chuck wagon and cooking tent. Kanti had been hired again. She would travel with and cook for the group Fred Stimson was heading up. Fred assigned a couple of younger riders to rotate day by day, helping with the gathering of firewood, peeling potatoes, bringing in some wild meat, and whatever else the cook needed to have done. The young fellows grumbled a bit, but they did the job anyway. Just being on the roundup was a reward in itself.

The entire roundup crew was fed together on the first morning, before setting out to their assigned stations. With no corrals or fence lines to tie horses to, the roping and saddling of all the mounts took some time. The melee caused by the reluctant horses created a dust cloud that drifted with the wind, directly towards the several cooking fires, and the many pots and frying pans loaded down with breakfast. The result was a loud outcry from the cooks and yelling from the assigned foremen to "Get those animals away from here."

The angry cooks' voices were interrupted by a shouted warning from a young rider atop a stomping, fishtailing, fighting, unruly gelding. With the horse completely out of control and the young rider trapped into a situation far beyond his ability, he was unable to turn the beast away from the cook fires. With much arm waving, shouting and foul language, the cooks, and a few other cowboys tried in vain to hold the bucking animal off.

With one fire spread in every direction and a big pot of coffee soaking into the ground, while the cook was reaching into the wagon for his carbine, the gelding finally found just the right move to unseat the unwelcome weight on his back. With three great lunges, his heels high in the air between each lunge, the gelding leaped several feet forward and then jammed his front hooves firmly into the grass. The young man lost his stirrups, missed his grab for the horn and sailed over the mount's head, landing in a painful pile on the prairie grass. Like magic, the gelding, now free of his rider, settled down and started grazing.

The rider managed to rise to his feet, looking for his hat and vainly trying to swipe the dirt off his face, and spit the grass out of his mouth.

As the men started gathering around, some to help the cooks get the fires back into usable order and others to take advantage of the remaining coffee pots, the gelding drifted towards John. From out of the crowd came the call, "Give him a try, John. If you can't settle him down, we'll shoot him. Stew him up for dinner, with a helping of gravy and a bucket of biscuits."

There was good natured laughter and a general shout of approval from the cowboys. Kanti came to the edge of the cooking area with a big revolver in her hand. Looking like she meant business, and knew how to back it up, she hollered, "You come here I shoot horse and black man too."

Someone else shouted, "Ride him, John. Just don't go near the grub pile again."

Giving in to temptation, John took two steps and closed on the grazing animal. He flipped the reins over the gelding's neck and, ignoring the stirrups, grabbed the horn, and with a thrust from his strong legs, leaped into the saddle. Men close by scattered in all directions. John found the stirrups and kicked his heels into the gelding's ribs. "You gonna give me de ride, horse, or you jest gonna stand dere?"

It was as if the question awoke the animal. With a series of leaps ending with his front hooves planted in the grass, followed by a series of jumps, where all four feet left the ground, the animal lowered his head and raised his rear quarters into the air, kicking out with his hind legs. On one leap the horse turned completely around and landed facing the crowd of cowboys. John could be heard to holler, "Come on, horse. You is suppose to be de bad boy. You ain't shown ol' John noth'n yet."

With his strong legs gripping the barrel of the horse, John removed his hat and repeatedly slapped the gelding's hip with it, all the time telling it to show its meanness. After two more small crow hops the gelding went into a full sunfishing jump. John hollered in joy and kept slapping with his hat. Finally, the horse settled his four feet on the ground and began running blindly, directly towards the Oldman River. The bank was low at that point. The horse half stumbled and then, at the last possible second, leaped into the river. Both horse and rider disappeared beneath the cold water.

The men rushed to the riverbank, startled

at this turn of events, and fearing for John's life. They needn't have been concerned. Within seconds there was a churning on the surface of the river and John's head appeared, then his body and then the horse. John swam the horse to the bank and kicked him up onto the level prairie. As soon as the horse had his feet back on solid ground John again started slapping with his hat. The animal didn't move, standing with his head down, dripping water onto the spring grass.

"You had enough has you, horse? I'm tink maybe-so you be a good horse now."

John wrung the water out of his hat and placed it back on his head. He stepped to the ground and passed the reins to the young man who was limping a bit after being bucked off a few minutes before.

"Maybe-so he be a good ride now."

The men stood in wondering silence, until someone hollered out, "That's the second bath you've taken in that river, John." John recognized the voice of Bill Moodie.

"Dat ol' river be jest as cold de second time, Bill."

To break up the early morning festivities, one of the cooks rolled a metal rod around the inside of an iron triangle. As the riders turned back to the cookfires, hoping something of the breakfast had survived the morning's activities, Fred pulled up beside John.

"That was quite a show, John. I'm not sure I'd recommend its repeat though."

John offered no response.

CHAPTER 9

Most of the men knew exactly what to do. They had been on roundups before. But, Fred Stimson ran over the plan anyway.

"You'll be in three groups, men. You have already been called out for your group. Your foremen have been assigned. Follow the chuck wagon to your working area. You know what to do after that. Good luck and good hunting."

First, the missing and wandering cattle had to be found and gathered together. That was no small job. With the huge acreage broken up between rising, treed foothills, to river valleys, to flat or rolling prairie, from grassland to riverside light forest, the cattle had no shortage of places to hide. That was especially true of the new mama cows who were intent on hiding their babies.

Each small gather would then be pushed towards the larger bunch. Eventually all three crews would drift their bunch into the center where all the brands would be sorted out, taking care to keep cows and calves together. The few dogie calves would be assigned to cover expenses, with each ranch being free to bid on their ownership.

Of the couple of dozen ranches holding ground in the vast area of southern Alberta, the Bar U was by far the largest. The Cochrane herd was nearly as numerous, at least before the winter storms had so devastatingly cut its numbers. Even so, the largest Cochrane bunch was far to the north, across the Bow and west of the growing village of Calgary. Only those Cochran's that were wintered south of the Bow and had somehow survived had wandered south along with the Bar U and the others. The roundup would have little to do with the Cochrane.

George had estimated one month for the completed roundup but, in fact, it was completed in three weeks. There was one more large communal meal enjoyed by the men. Some of them wouldn't be meeting again for months. Some would never meet again. There was much laughing and story-telling and teasing, all in a futile attempt to push aside any personal feelings for each other that might hint of emotion or caring.

The caring was there, without a doubt. Not a man existed among the bunch who wouldn't saddle up, risking life and limb, at a call for assistance, or a mention of trouble.

The drive back to the Bar U took another week. By that time the carpenters had the original log structure closed in and ready for the men. The crude fire-blackened rock ring that had staved off the worst of the cold the previous winter, had been replaced with a metal, wood burning stove. There would be no more freezing, shivering nights for the riders of the North West Cattle Company.

CHAPTER 10

True to Fred Stimson's judgement and
prediction, John proved to have itchy feet.
With the cattle driven home to the Bar U
from the roundup, the calves branded, and
the entire herd counted, Fred wrote a long
report to the Allan Brothers, back in Montreal. Although Fred was manager and part
owner of the North West Cattle Company,
the Allans, as majority bankers and backers
still required regular reports on the happenings with the ranch. With no railway in place
yet, the mail would go by horseback or
stagecoach to Fort Benton, down in Montana. From there it would make its slow way
east on a Missouri river boat and then, by
whatever means were available, across the
long miles to Montreal. Or they may send it
south to intersect with the rail line somewhere in Nebraska.

With the rails nearing Calgary, soon the
mail would travel in just a few days, across

the wide continent.

It was a sad duty to report on the losses of Bar U animals, as well as the even more devastating losses to other brands. The Cochrane herd was decimated through poor management and unpreparedness. Thawing, rotting and stinking carcasses were a common sight across much of the land. All that, and more, would go into Fred's report.

With the long summer days ahead of them, the workers were assigned the tasks that were designed to enhance the growth of the Bar U. Fred went from man to man, first thanking them for their faithfulness and stalwartness during the truly miserable winter months. He then laid out the work to be done during the summer. When he came to John, he said, "John, I've thanked you before, but I want to thank you again. You proved yourself a man, in every sense of that word during the past few months. A man I'm proud to work with and, I hope, to call friend. Now, with the warm weather ahead of us I would like you to be back with the horses. I'd like you to gather them up and check them over carefully. You will need to pay special attention to their fee. Some will have common problems with skin diseases, and such. The winter was hard on the animals. Then there will be foals that

need to be branded and gelded come wean-
ing time. Well, I know I'm just talking, saying things you already know."

Fred was about to go on about horse matters on the ranch, but John interrupted.

"Boss, I's got ta thank you for de good offer. But I be leav'n in de morn'n. Ol' Tom
he want'n me ta ride south fer ta drive
'nother bunch a cattle up ta here. But Smith
from down ta de Crossing, he speak first
an' say he got a summer job fer ol' John. I
promise I come see him after de roundup
be finished. Maybe-so I be back by n by
Boss. Be look'n fer de winter's work. I come
an' see you den."

Fred couldn't keep the disappointment
from showing on his face or sounding in his
voice.

"Why, John, I thought you knew there was
a permanent position here for you. You have
no need of searching for work. If it's a matter of wages perhaps we could find some
way to make an offer."

"Not be de wages, Boss. Jest be de want'n
to see new places an do de new things. Jest
want'n ta see de new country. Dat be why I
left Fort Worth. I be want'n to see de country."

Late the following evening, John stood with

Smith, at The Crossing, as the two men surveyed the row of sticks driven into the prairie sod, outlining the path the new irrigation ditch was to follow.

"You will always be able to say you were the first to dig an irrigation ditch in Alberta, John. That's the summer's work I have for you. You and this new fella. Dan by name. He'll be along come morning. There's shovels and a couple of wheelbarrows back in the shed. You just walk yourselves along that row of sticks, from this here garden patch. You'll see the stakes lead off towards the river. All you fellas have to do is start at the river and dig your way back to the garden. Don't need a big ditch, maybe just double the width of a shovel blade. You'll see from the low riverbank how deep you need to dig. We ain't trying to create no flood here. Just enough flow to irrigate the garden. We'll build a gate at the river's edge before you open up those last few feet. Got to have some control, you know."

The next morning John and Dan stood together, shovels in hand staring at the river's edge. Dan looked at John with a whimsical but resigned look on his face.

"I'm not sure this is exactly what I had in mind during all those years of studying, John. Nor what I visualized when I boarded the train back east. Mind you, since the trains aren't quite ready for regular passenger runs yet, I worked my way west on the rails, doing some jobs that were not so much different from this.

"Still, it's more likely I had visions of riding and romance. You know, the cowboy life. There's lots of folks writing up the romance and excitement of cowboying on the big ranches. Never doing any work that can't be done from the back of a horse, and all that stuff. And here I stand with a shovel in my hand and a long patch of digging before me. I'll do it though. I made a promise. And Smith's money will spend as good as anyone else's, I suppose."

John thought about that statement for a few seconds before answering, "I be work'n on de ranches and driv'n de cows for some years now, Dan. Sometimes be exciting when de horse's not want'n ta be rode. Sometimes be terrible hot. Sometimes be cold. Cold ta de bone. De grass bed not ever be soft. Most of de meals be not so good. De days be longer dan de light be shin'n and de cows, dey be not very smart. Get inta every kind a trouble.

"But I go back to de cows after dis water be flown onta de garden, jest de same."

The two men stood there in silence for

another half minute before Dan said, "Well, my new friend, why don't you take the first shovel full. I'll follow along and clean out what you leave behind. I'm guessing we'll never finish if we don't ever start."

Without comment John sank his shovel in, full depth of the blade, opening the prairie sod on the bank of the Highwood River for the first time.

Those who had a calendar could see for themselves that the next page said, 'September'. The ditch was completed. John and Dan had allowed just enough water to flow to prove the slope was correct, but not enough to peel the newness off the project. That privilege would be left for Smith or French.

Smith and French both walked with Dan and John to where the irrigation gate had been built at the edge of the Highwood River. The gate was a simple wooden affair. No more than a few short boards nailed together and fitted into a slot in the side frames. Smith, never a man of emotion or much of a sense of history, simply bent over and gripped the handle that had been fashioned onto the gate. Without ceremony, he lifted it up and grunted with satisfaction as the river water made its way down the ditch.

John and Dan looked on with considerable satisfaction. The new flow duplicated their quick test run the day before.

Smith celebrated the momentous occasion by saying, "Ain't about to do much good for the garden this late in the year, but we got big hopes for spring. Come to the store. I have your money ready for you."

Dan looked at the unfeeling man as he turned back to his collection of shacks, and then glanced at John, remembering the days of hard work, the sore muscles and the sweat that had gone into the past few weeks. Both men burst into laughter at the ridiculous, almost callous words of their employer. But they picked up their shovels and followed along, to gather in their pay.

CHAPTER 11

"What's your plan now, John?"

"I'm head'n back to the Bar U, Dan. I promised Mr. Stimson I be happy to work fo him for de winter. Got de new bunk house finished and all be ready for de riders. I's hop'n ta be outta de cold an wind fer dis winter. What yo goin' be do'n Dan?"

"I'm not altogether sure on that, John. French keeps talking about going in search of gold in the spring. I believe I might join him. You could come along if you wished. But for now, I think I'm going to catch the stage and ride up to Calgary. I'm told it's grown and changed even in the few months since I was there last. I'm hoping you have a good winter, John. Maybe we'll get together again in the spring."

The two men shook hands and John went to saddle his horse.

The winter months passed slowly on the Alberta grasslands. As usual, what little bit of news arriving at the ranches was spread from one rider to another, from one ranch to another. Stories were circulated of bitter cold nights on the grasslands when a crew was caught unawares, away from shelter; of the struggle to pull cattle from snow drifts; of the miserably hard work of calving during the cold of early spring; of desperately hungry Natives taking a steer here, a growing yearling there; and of the ranchers that allowed them to do it; of new, totally unprepared ranches being set up. On and on the stories went.

But as spring came the big story making the rounds was of the exploit put together by Frank Strong and some riders he had gathered around him.

Fred Stimson, who had recently returned from The Crossing was holding court in the cook house.

"Most likely you've all heard about the Cochrane herd being driven south last fall. Some of you maybe saw it making its way through a corner of our grasslands."

The men sitting around the combination cook house and dining room on the Bar U listened as the tale was told. There was always time for 'end of the day' story telling on the lonely frontier.

"After the disaster on their ranch west of

Calgary, during that terrible storm we all suffered through last winter, the Cochrane, determined to avoid another such happening, made an additional questionable management decision.

"They drove their herd south, hoping to keep the cattle and the ranch alive, should it come to where we have another killing winter. Didn't turn out as they had hoped. Now, thankfully, we've had a fairly easy time of it up here on the Highwood this past winter. Chinooks enough, and decent grazing. Of course, most had some hay set by too, as we had. But we could never put up anywhere near enough to hold the growth on a herd as big as the Bar U bunch. We mainly put up the hay to keep those expensive eastern bulls in working condition.

"The news the stage driver brought down to Smith's place is that the Cochrane should have kept their animals to home. Apparently, the snow was light up north and the chinooks frequent enough. It was not so down south.

"The news from down south, west of Macleod, is that the Cochrane animals found themselves trapped in a hopeless snowfall. The grass was covered by a couple of feet of the white stuff. No possibility of graze or water, either one. There seemed to be nothing at all that the riders could do. Nothing but admit their mistake and wish they could push back the clock, as they watched the poor, suffering beasts starve, withering towards death. The cattle couldn't push through the snow and the riders had no idea where they might find grass anyway. It looked like the end of the herd. And of the Cochrane ranch."

The Bar U men glanced at one another, remembering the troubles they had lived through the first hard winter. Each man, if put to it, could still feel the cold in his feet and the despair in his heart as he watched the poor suffering cattle standing miserably in the deep snow. But the worst of the memories was the sight of dead animals piled one atop another in some little coulee or stream bed, where the wind had driven, and then trapped them.

"Now, I say it looked like the end of the ranch, and I guess the Cochrane thought so too. They put out a reward offer for anyone that could save the day. Turns out Frank Strong came up with an idea and accepted the challenge."

The men perked up as that statement was made. Knowing the hopeless feeling of trying to care for stranded cattle, and wondering what they themselves might have done, they listened intently to the solution Frank Strong came up with.

"What he did was, he and some of his riders gathered up a large herd of horses, some from around Fort Macleod but most from the Blackfoot Tribes. Some are saying there was five hundred head, but no one heard that number directly from Frank. In fact, those that know are saying Frank has moved on to other matters and isn't saying much at all. Seems to be content to have the facts speak for themselves without more words from him.

"As you know, horses are strong on their feet. They handle the snow better than cattle do. Where a cow critter will flounder to a stop, lost and bawling his fool head off, a horse will simply push through. That's what Frank's plan was depending on.

"He drove those hundreds of horses right out to where the Cochrane was dying. Left a trail of trampled down and broken snow drifts behind them that anyone could follow. Those boys gathered up the cattle. Herded them onto the horse-broke trail and followed the horses as they returned to the Fort, trampling the snow down even more as they went along. Drove them right out to good grass graze, following that broken trail. Saved the herd and pocketed a nice bundle of Cochrane cash in the process."

One of the cowboys listening in said, "Ain't it truly amazing what ideas a fella can come up with when the need is upon him?"

Fred nodded in agreement as he looked over at the speaker.

"Fellas, I'll tell you. I've said it before, and I'll say it again. There are men on this range, and in this room, who will be written down in the history books. True pioneers, each one. Men who are making a difference. Outstanding men. Men for the times. Men who are figuring it all out, often leaning on lessons learned elsewhere. This isn't the only cold cattle country. Things learned in another place often just have to be gathered up and adapted to the current situation.

"All through history there have been men, and women both, who have made a difference in their day. On this womanless frontier it's men, for now. The women will come in a year or two, and we'll all be the better for it. They'll be strong women, for no other could survive and thrive out here. Some of them, too, will be spoken about a century from now. Some of you sitting here will be among those leaders that go down in history."

Fred was enjoying his reminiscing and his

predictions of the future. He didn't often have an audience like this. Nor had he ever shown this side of his thinking.

"Look around you as you go about your days. See what's happening and who's doing it. Pick good leaders and follow them. Whether school children know our names in fifty years, or not, know inside yourselves that you're helping to build a nation. Take pride in that. Frank Strong is just one of many that are worthy of being followed."

The crew sat in silence for a short while, most of them lifting their coffee cups to their mouths, hoping to find another drop or two in the bottom. The last man to visit the pot on the big kitchen wood range had proclaimed it as empty as he slid it off the heat.

"What's next on the U, Fred?"

Fred Stimson glanced over at the man who had asked the question and said, "A general roundup. That's what's new, Herb. It's a caution how many new folks there are on the range. Can't imagine where they all came from in so short a period of time. Ranches about everywhere grass grows, cattle by the thousands, and every head of them running loose.

"I'm concerned on two counts. First is that some of our cows are making friends with some pretty rangy looking bulls. Can't grow a quality herd that way. And it's quality the eastern market has always been looking for. They've accepted whatever was shipped their way just to satisfy their growing market but now they're becoming more particular. The days of marketing longhorn beeves that have to be cut with a hatchet are over.

"We went to all the trouble and expense of bringing in good breeding bulls for the Bar U. We need to keep our herd close and the rangy stuff away if we're ever going to get the benefit of those bulls.

"Then, while I expect that every man holding down a brand is basically honest, yet temptation can raise its ugly head where it was least expected. Every man wants to grow his brand as fast as nature will allow. Our cattle wander over a sight of land out there. Both men and animals are often alone, miles from where any outside eyes can see them. Should a wandering calf or two, or three, find itself under the wrong branding iron, well who's to know? Some few rancher's cows might have set a new world record on the births of twins.

"We haven't set ourselves up as guardians of the Alberta range but by jinks, we plan to be guardians of the Bar U range and its stock. You men take note. I don't ever want to hear that another man's animal is wearing the Bar U. I won't tolerate that. But I won't tolerate another man's brand on a Bar U animal either. Don't you be losing sight of either of those facts."

The men glanced at one another as the seriousness of Fred's pronouncement sank in. Every man there had witnessed the questionable claims made on weaned or near weaned calves on other open range territories. The issue had often developed to the shooting stage. No one would benefit if this, so far peaceful range, was turned into just another lawless battleground.

"We'll go in force to the roundup. We'll push no other man out of his place, but we'll not be pushed either. We'll gather up our bunch and drive them to their home range on the Highwood. I expect most of the others will be doing the same. This country is too big to allow animals to run wherever the wind drifts them, hoping to find them again someday."

Phil Weinard spoke up. "Are you talking fencing, Fred?"

That question brought about an uncomfortable shuffling of feet and several stiff looks as the men waited anxiously for the answer.

"Men, I know how most of you feel about barb wire. I feel much the same myself. This untouched range, grass waving in the wind for miles in every direction, from the mountains to the eastern flat lands, was a glorious sight when I first cast eyes on it. It still is, for the most part. I never have to wonder why the Indians loved it so much and why they fought the other tribes for it.

"The land is truly magnificent. I can only imagine what it must have looked like, not so many years ago, with the tens of thousands of buffalo, migrating through the country.

"It was as if God had just finished with His creation when I first saw this country. There wasn't a blemish anywhere. Now, I said it was glorious and that's exactly what it was. Will it stay that way? To do so there will have to be some kind of controls. Will the ranchers control themselves, not holding more hungry animals than their range can support? We can only hope. Will the homesteaders, when they start coming, leave the grasslands alone? Again, we can only hope. But if it takes barb wire to protect Bar U range and cattle, then barb wire is what we will have.

"There's grasslands down in Montana that may never again grow anything but weeds and cactus. Overgrazed right into a near enough desert. Grazed to the roots, and hooved down to gather up even the roots by hungry cattle. Unlimited, uncontrolled growth may sound fine, may even sound like freedom to do what you want, when you're sitting around drinking coffee, counting your wealth by the number of head carrying your brand. It isn't until a wise rancher sees what those many hooves are doing to his land, and he starts to look into the future, that he opens his eyes to see the devastation.

"It's tempting, when you see untouched grasslands in every direction, to convince yourself that it will last forever. But then you look on the result in other areas, and you realize it would be best you do some serious thinking.

"It's true that every man on this range is, at heart, a freedom loving man. I'd make that claim for myself as well. I left a good business back east. Slept in a warm bed every night. Ate the best of food. Rode only for a Sunday afternoon outing. Kept company with some lovely ladies. But as good as that sounds and, indeed, it was good, when I first cast an eye on this country, I was hooked. I knew I was home and all that back east was, in truth, frivolous.

118

"We can't let our carelessness destroy what has been sitting here for thousands of years."

Fred took his last sip of cold coffee and looked over the roomful of riders. Perhaps the time was right to continue, to explain the need for breeding and brand control.

"It's getting late but let me explain this one more thing. There's the matter of the range bulls running wherever they wish with no control from their owners. And the further matter of the weeks of hard riding it takes to find and gather our animals. Neither of those leads to good, responsible ranch management.

"That will eventually lead to fencing. But for now, it should be enough that we keep our animals close to home. That means days of riding the perimeter for you boys. But in return it means fewer miles to run weight off our stock and it means an easier gather for the Bar U when another springtime rolls around.

"And I should add that along with keeping our stock at home, we'll be driving all other stock off."

Another rider ventured, "That all sounds good, Boss, but it might be a bit more difficult than it sounds. The longhorn is a fast walking, determined critter. Never seems to be content in one place. Take a lot of riders to cover all this land and hold those animals to their home grass."

"Well, of course, you're right, Duncan. But the longhorn is dying out. Most of the animals brought up from Montana are crosses. Very few pure longhorns. Those crosses are losing their long legs and putting on a bit more beef. And as they cross with good bulls they'll move ever more in that direction. In another five years there won't be a longhorn left in Alberta.

"And to make sure the ranchers are protecting the grass, the Canadian government has inspectors on the ground, watching. And they're working closely with the NWMP. The government boys have seen the Montana range. They're determined it will be different in Canada. And so far, it is. The Bar U will do its part in keeping it that way.

"They're watching the tick problem too. Ticks haven't been too big an issue here yet because of the distances between ranches and the fact that there's not many domestic cattle to infect, and most folks keep their milk cows at home.

"Anyway, that's enough of that for this one evening. Now get yourselves off to your

bunks. We leave first thing in the morning
for Macleod."

CHAPTER 12

After the spring roundup, John rode to The Crossing. Still admitting to considerable doubt, and remembering his disaster on the Virginia City, Montana, gold show, but answering to some internal urging he wouldn't have been able to explain, he headed off on a gold seeking venture with Dan Riley and French. They returned months later with stories to tell, but no gold. John, a bit embarrassed by the entire matter, and avoiding the pointless miles that would take him back to The Crossing, bid 'farewell' to his gold seeking partners, turned off, and went back to the Bar U. After a short stay at the ranch, he rode again to The Crossing.

The Crossing was now being called High River by some, urged on by George Emerson, who was still promoting the concept of a town. John stepped down at the Smith and French holdings and tied his horse to the railing. Seeing activity across the river, where it swung to the south before looping back east again and then north, he took a few steps to the side so he could see past the old, tumble-down Smith and French establishment. Several new buildings had gone up. A lot of work had been done in the months since he had last visited. And he could see two or three still under way, their fresh-cut, white lumber gleaming in the fall sun. He lifted his ragged hat and scratched his curly hair in wonder. A voice sounded from behind him.

"So, what do you make of all that, John?"

John turned to see his ditch digging and gold hunting partner Dan, grinning at him.

"Where all dees folks, dey come from, Dan? Looks like dey be build'n a sure enough town over der."

"That's exactly what they're doing, John. Tough competition for Smith and French. I rode over on the new ferry a couple of days ago. Took a look around. Talked to some folks.

"That two-story building you see going up is a hotel. The one beside it is a restaurant. Further down is a barn and livery. The big building beside the barn is going to be a mercantile store. There's no stopping it now. With the rails bringing folks to Calgary from the east, sometimes two train loads of them each week, all looking for opportunity, often enough meaning land or business, this country is going to boom. You'd better grab your piece while you can, John."

"Dat's why I be here Dan. I's goin ketch de stage fer de big city. I's goin file on a piece of land. Got me a nice one all picked out. Was goin ta leave de horse here wit Smith. Maybe-so I take it over ta de barn."

Dan toed some prairie dust into the air as if he was struggling with a decision. He studied his friend and said, "I really should be going with you. I've been enjoying this pioneer life the past couple of years but really, I'm a city man and I know it. That's where I'll end up, come the right time."

There was a momentary pause before Dan said, "Aw shucks, John, I guess I'll give this life another little while anyway. I'll wish you luck and see you when you get back. But before you go, I have to ask, what do you think about the gold hunting, now that you've had a bit of time to mull on it?"

He had a huge grin on his face as he said it.

"Dan, Ol' John not ever agin wish'n ta go ta look fer de gold. Down ta Montana an' Idaho I come near ta freeze an' starve, look'n fer de gold. Didn't know what was goin' get me first, de hunger or de cold. And dis place we go fer de gold, it be full a de haunts an sech. An no gold. Ol' John he be stay'n wit' de cows 'n' de horses from here."

There was no grin on John's face or any sign that he was jesting.

Dan clapped him on the shoulder and said, "French wants me to go with him again. I told him he'd best find someone else to enjoy his company on the next trip."

CHAPTER 13

The short stage ride to Calgary took John through open range land with a few cattle in sight but not a single building. The trail then entered into the hill country as the land began forming the basis for the Bow and Elbow River valleys. John didn't know quite how to express his thoughts on what he was seeing but he spoke aloud to the other stage riders anyway, "Dis be a sure enough purty country."

The response from the three other passengers was silence until one grizzled and odiferous young fella who looked like he'd maybe spent the summer in the hills, perhaps hunting gold or, more likely just wandering, seeing a new land before it became old, spoke through a face of tangled and filthy hair, "A lot of pretty country up this way. Me? I prefer the high up forests, just sitting by a glacier melt stream, wishing within me that it could always stay this way but knowing that it won't."

The self-important man sitting right beside the speaker ventured, "Not to be overly impolite, young fella, but life on this stage ride would be a bit more agreeable if you had perhaps taken advantage of the many qualities of that water you were sitting beside."

Knowing he was referring to bathing, or the lack thereof, the bearded youth turned his head and looked directly into the eyes of the critic. Both men appeared to be holding their positions until the youth broke into a wide grin. The facial change was barely visible through the tangle of beard but the crinkling around his eyes spoke of good humor. He held his stare for another few seconds before turning again, addressing John.

"Not many dark-skinned fellas up this way. I'm guessing you've seen some country and ridden some miles to have arrived on this frontier. Are you a cowboy, a wanderer or a well-disguised man of letters, sir?"

"Ol' John don't know what dis man of letters be. Ain't never heard of sech as that. But I's sure been rid'n some miles. Rid'n from Sout' Carolina te Fort Worth. Dat be in Texas. Move de cows from Fort Worth ta dis place. Work'n on de ranches fo' more den ten years. I's cowboy enough I s'pose."

The self-important traveler asked, "And what would be attracting a dark-skinned fella, as this man referred to you, to Calgary? I don't know as there will be much opportunity for such as you in the city."

The bearded young man turned again and flashed his grin at the speaker. Clearly, he wasn't one to be intimidated, no matter the status of his riding companion. When he had thoroughly stared down the man he said, "I suppose, sir, that you have a name. Would you mind sharing it?"

There was a long period with only the shout of the driver and the clattering of the steel rimmed wheels breaking the silence in the dust filled stage. Finally relenting, and puffed up with pride, the man said, "I, sir, am Mortimer L. Alphonse, attorney at law, if you insist on knowing. You may refer, if you must refer to me at all, as Mr. Alphonse."

The grinning young man shifted the rifle he held upright between his knees and said, "Well, you see how friendly that can be? You're Mortimer and this man has already called himself John, so all that's missing in this triangle of conversational fellowship and learning, that the man beside John is wisely avoiding, is my name. My parents, and yes sir, I really did, and still do, have parents, named me, if you can believe it, Aloysius Graton Havener. Now what kind of a loving father would hang an appellation like that on an unsuspecting and defenseless child? No, it simply wouldn't do. I rebelled at a young age and named myself Buddy. Or simply Bud if the former is too much to remember."

The solicitor seemed to shrink before John's eyes. He said nothing for a slow count of five and then sputtered, "You are Mr. Havener?"

"Why yes, Mortimer. I am. I suspect you have come west at my bidding."

Bud seemed to be enjoying the other man's discomfort.

The sputtering continued as the flustered man said, "Yes. Yes. I did. On my enquiry in Calgary, they said you had gone to Fort Macleod. That I could most likely find you there. Obviously, I did not. I was heading back to Calgary on this horribly dusty and uncomfortable conveyance, in hopes of locating you. But I must say, I was not expecting . . . I mean I wasn't looking . . ."

Bud finished the stumbling lawyer's sentence for him. "What you mean to say, Mortimer, is that you were not looking for someone such as myself. Well, that, at least, is understandable. Perhaps it would set your Eastern mind at ease if I assured you that I clean up pretty good."

John had lost interest in the verbal exchange and was contenting himself with a study of the rolling hills, until Buddy said, "What you see here, John, right before your well-travelled eyes, is the perfect and complete demonstration of an Easterner making his first trip into this glorious and free land, bringing his Eastern ways with him."

Turning back to the lawyer he continued, "It simply won't do, Mortimer. Won't do at all. This land is too large, too grand, too powerful, to be impressed by Eastern bluff and bluster. You will bend to this land, Mortimer, and be the better for it, or the land will break you, and you'll be on the train headin back to the big smoky city with your tail between your legs.

"But before you go, I have a piece of work for you to complete. That work has to do with the CPR, a railway that is rapidly becoming known as a veritable magnet of lawsuits.

"I have a room held for me at the Royal Hotel. The hotel doesn't amount to much at this early date but there will be better offerings before long, I'm quite sure of that. I will make myself available to you at seven this evening in the dining room. We may discuss our business then. In the meantime, I suggest that you spend your time observing and learning and keeping your opinions of the West under wraps. There are some who are quite possessive of this West. You would not want to run afoul of a man of that nature.

"As a start in your long learning process, I would argue that John here has accomplished, starting from a position of disadvantage that neither you nor I can hope to understand, more than most of the city people you have ever met. You may want to think on that."

John thought Buddy had said a good thing, but he wasn't altogether sure. There had been a lot of words strung together, with his name among them. Turning back to his appreciation of what nature had provided in the landscape, he found himself eager to get his homestead filed and return to The Crossing, putting the city behind him.

Stepping from the stage in front of the Royal Hotel, the passengers stretched and groaned as they worked out the kinks and sore spots gathered over the hours of stage travel. John, with a single thought on his mind was determined to find the land of-

131

fice, where he could point out the quarter section he had chosen for his future home.

With the Quirks' smiling approval, John, months ago, had secreted the leather pouch that contained his considerable savings, in a spot he hoped would remain his secret, on the welcoming couple's small ranch. On his way to The Crossing, he had ridden to the Quirks for a visit. He had also retrieved his pouch and dug out some coins. Now he was carrying enough money, pushed deeply into his pants pocket, for the land filing, a couple of meals and a stage ride back to The Crossing. If he had to sleep over, he planned to enquire at the livery for loft space.

Having no idea where to look for the land office, he began wandering. Although the town was certainly growing, with buildings going up in every direction he looked, it was still small compared to Fort Worth or Memphis or even Cheyenne. He smiled inwardly as he thought back to when he had entered the first unknown village on his ride up from South Carolina. At the time he was overwhelmed with the size of the settlement. Now, seeing it in his memory for what it really was, he was amazed and a bit embarrassed that he had been so ignorant, that he had known so little of the world.

Perhaps the fella lounging on the questionable comfort of the poplar log railing at the livery corral recognized a rider in John. Possibly the hat, the worn canvas pants, the neck scarf and the mannerisms were enough to alert the young man to who or what John was. He spoke, drawing John to a stop.

"Help ya, mister? You're look'n kind a lost. Jest seen ya gett'n off the stage. First time in the big city of Calgary?"

John turned towards the voice and pulled off his hat, wringing it in his strong fingers, a habit that showed his nervousness.

"Yass'r, Boss, I's need ta find de land office. Kin you point it out ta me?"

"You'll have no trouble find'n it. Just look over your shoulder. It's that shack down the road a piece. The one with those fellas hang'n around the front. But I'm duty bound to warn you to be careful."

"I's jest goin sign up for de homestead. Den git back ta de ranch. What fo I got ta be careful?"

The fence sitter made John wait for an answer while he completed the rolling of a cigarette, licked and sealed it, and then, first studying his handiwork, put it in his mouth and pulled a match across the seat of his jeans, holding the fire to the end of the cigarette. He took a satisfying drag, blew out the smoke and studied John.

"I expect you ain't heard of the hanging."

"No sir. I never heard of no hang'n."

Again, the cowboy drew smoke into his lungs while he studied John.

"Fella murdered a while back. Bad situation, little place like this. Didn't know the man myself. But, it seems, most people counted him as a friend. At least they did after he was dead. Don't know how they felt about him before that time.

"Blame was laid on the only black man in town. Man name of Jesse Williams. Kind of a catchy name, that. Someone should write a song about him. No real proof that he really done it, so far as I've ever heard. But they gave him a trial and everything before they hung him. First man to have the honor of hanging in the whole territory. Should go down in the history books. So now there's two men dead and no good feelings at all towards fellas sporting a darker hue of complexion such as yourself. I ain't judging you, friend, but I repeat, you'd best go careful. Do what you came to do and get yourself back on that stage and back to the ranch."

John was shaken to the core. He was feeling the first real threat since leaving South Carolina. He studied the young man on the corral fence and said, "I be thank'n you fo

134

de warn'n. Ol' John sure don't be want'n no trouble. I be careful."

He started to walk away when an idea came into his mind. He turned back to the young rider and asked, "You be look'n fo de rid'n job? Always seem ta be more riders needed on de Bar U. Down ta de Cross'n. Maby you rid'n down dat way come by n by."

"Maby I will, John. Ya, I just might do that."

John walked slowly towards the land office, carefully watching the small gathering of men on the boardwalk outside. Although there were a few hard stares, no one tried to prevent him from entering the office. But inside, he ran into a problem he hadn't anticipated. With the help of the clerk, he studied the map of the land around The Crossing and carefully placed his finger on the chosen site.

"That's the homestead you want is it, fella?"

"Yes, sir Boss, dat be de one."

The clerk turned the map towards himself so he could read the legal description and started filing out the application form.

"Who am I making this out for?"

"I be John, sir."

"John what? What is your last name?"

"Ah be jest John, sir."

"I can't assign you a homestead without you giving me your full legal name. John alone won't do. You must have a last name. Everyone has."

John had struggled for all the months since telling Tom Lynch what his slave family name was. No one had asked his name since that day, except Fred Stimson, so the subject lay in sullen secrecy. In truth, he had no solid reason for not using it, and he had no assurance that either Tom or Fred hadn't been speaking his name to others. But that he connected it in his mind with the slave farm couldn't be denied. Perhaps he was going to have to get over those old angers and fears.

But now. What to do now? He treasured his secret, but did he want that land more than he wanted to keep the name secret? He hesitated, studying the land agent all the while, hoping to see some sign of relenting in the man's eyes.

After riding away from the slave farm, he had vowed to himself that he would never again use the name the owner thrust upon his family. He had reluctantly yielded the information just the once, after his conversation with Tom Lynch on the ride north, admitting to being John Ware, when he

136

signed on to ride for the Bar U.

What if he simply made up a name? Who could ever know? His thoughts were interrupted by the clerk clearing his throat and asking again, "Your full name sir?"

John choked down his pride and said, "Ware, sir. My name be John Ware."

The clerk ventured no opinion on the name or the chosen land. He simply completed the form, asked John to sign, and was ready to complete the transaction. John was forced to admit that he could neither read nor write.

The clerk passed John the pen and said, "Good many out here in the same situation, John. You're not the first to enter this office. You just put your X right there. I'll sign as witness, and you'll have your homestead."

John followed the man's instructions, paid over the few dollars asked, and received the piece of paper offered as proof of possession. Ownership wouldn't be final until John proved up on the site.

He folded the single-page document and folded it into his shirt pocket. After thanking the clerk, he made his way back to the livery corral, where the young rider was now standing on the outside, leaning back against the rough poplar rails. He was again rolling a cigarette.

"Got er done did ya?"

"Yassir, I got de paper right here." He patted his pocket with a broad grin on his face.

John and the young man, who now named himself as 'Sid', went to a small eating house and had supper together, and then made their way back to the livery.

John paid for passage to The Crossing for the next morning as they passed the stage office. After a long, cool, fall evening, visiting with Sid, and a longer night trying for comfort in the hayloft, John was back on the stage and headed home. This time he picked up his horse from the stable and rode out to his chosen homestead, looking forward to gathering enough logs to put up his first shelter.

CHAPTER 14

After doing the backbreaking work of cutting, trimming and hauling logs from the
river flats to his building site, John was
exhausted. He and his horse, both. And
winter was coming on, which is no small
matter on the Alberta plains. He could
clearly see there was no possibility of him
getting a roof over his head before the first
snow fall. So, when Fred Stimson rode up
to the site on his return from The Crossing,
with an invitation for John to work out the
winter on the Bar U, he accepted, remembering the warm bunkhouse and the regular
meals. He could get back to his homestead
in the spring.

But by the spring of 1885 much was happening around the country. Under the
shadow of native and Metis unrest at far-off
Duck Lake, the spring roundup proceeded
with one eye ever glancing to the northeast,
fearing unhappy news. The talk of war on

the prairies seemed to force its way into every other conversation.

Fred Stimson approached the men who were gathered around the bunkhouse and cook shack, readying themselves for the day's work. He singled out John.

"Are you coming to roundup, John, or you going back to hauling logs? I swear, when I saw you last fall, I'm not sure who was working the hardest, you or your horse. Might be a sight easier on the body if you were to ride roundup. And we could sure use you."

"Yassir, Boss, I figure ta come ta de roundup. Be good ta meet up with some of de fellas again. I'll git back ta build'n my house after dat."

Not much time had passed since the first small roundup but already the ranches were putting a bit of showmanship into their preparations. It was a trend that was to last through time, in the district. Calgary and the south country would be the parade, rodeo and celebration center of the western plains, led by a few men who had yet to arrive in the area.

The Bar U was no exception in the trend towards showmanship. Fred had his brand arrive on the roundup grounds with wagons, cook tent, sleeping tent and the largest crew on the prairies. Although underneath, he was all business, he enjoyed the idea of riding at the head of the cavalcade, letting everyone know that the Bar U, second to none on the Alberta grass, had arrived.

Fred called his crew together at the end of the first day. Standing beside him was a lithe, competent looking young fella who had ridden in from the south that day.

"Men, I wish you'd say hello to George Lane. I'm getting busier than I want to be, so I brought George in as foreman of the Bar U. I won't call out all your names right now. You can shake hands with George as opportunity presents itself. I have to head back up to The Crossing. I'll be leaving in the morning. George will take over our part of the roundup. I'm trusting that you will work as well with George as you have for me and that all will go well. We'll see you back at the ranch in a while."

There was much mumbling among the gathered men but none of it mattered to John. Although he knew full well that he could run the crew and the roundup both, and do just fine at the task, he was expecting no such trust or privilege. If one or two of the other riders had wanted the job, that had nothing to do with him.

As happens in every roundup there were

weaned calves with considerable growth on them but no brand. The roundup association had, since the beginning, insisted that unbranded, weaned calves would become general property, available for purchase by any ranch that wanted them, with the proceeds going to the association to cover costs. Although there was some minor resentment towards this action, the association prevailed.

John spoke quietly to his friend John Quirk. "John, I's goin' ta buy me some of dem calves. I got de brand registered. I's be us'n de four nines, de 9999 brand. Maybe ten, twelve o' dem be mine at de end a de roundup. What you tink a dat, John?"

His friend was slow to answer but his smile spoke for him before the words did.

"Why I think that's great, John. It's a small start but by hang, it's a start. You could turn them out with my bunch. That might hold them in one place. And who knows what might come of it? I expect you'll have a ranch of your own when the timing is right."

John thanked his friend and went back to take his place on night herding. Bill Moodie rode up beside him and threw his leg over the saddle horn, reaching for his tobacco pouch.

"Quiet tonight, John. I'd be just as happy if it stayed that way. I hope I'm not just getting old, but I find the more peaceful things are, the better I like it."

John watched his friend build his cigarette, a habit he had never taken on himself. When the paper and tobacco were rolled and lit, with Bill blowing a puff of smoke and watching it disappear into the wind, John said, "Peaceful out here on de grass, a' right. But maybe-so not so peaceful other places. Der be lots a horse steal'n by de Indians. Ranch horses and de horses from other Indians down ta Montana. Police say dat could maybe make de big Indian war. Dat be bad fer everyone. Den I'm hear'n of de Indians, dey be unhappy at de place called Duck Lake. I don' know where dat is but Fred say it could maybe be real war."

"What you've heard is true, John. Fred is organizing a Ranger force to patrol the foothills, hoping to protect the ranch horses, and the cattle, both. The stealing across the border will have to be dealt with by the Mounties and the American army. I sure hope that doesn't flare up into something that can't be controlled. And the Duck Lake thing sounds troublesome too. A lot of these riders you see here plan to join other Ranger groups to head up there after roundup. I don't know what the issues are, but any time government gets involved things can only get worse.

"Then, the ranches, including the Bar U are concerned because homesteaders can now legally claim plots of land inside the ranch lease areas. It doesn't make much sense to me but there it is, anyway. If the homesteaders claim the river accesses and the waterholes, the ranches will be in big trouble. That could easily lead to violence."

After the two men sat in silence for a while, thinking on these things, John smiled at his friend and said, "Maybe-so none of des things be happen, Bill. Maybe-so all be alright on dis grass."

"Maybe-so, John. It could be you are right. Maybe-so it will all blow away on the wind."

CHAPTER 15

Foreman George Lane walked up beside John as he was readying his horse for a ride to Calgary. One ride on the bumpy, dusty stage had been enough for him.

"I'm told you're heading up to Calgary, John. What's drawing you to the big city? You know there's a job for you here. I'd like it if you'd stay with us."

"I 'preciate dat, Boss, but I's goin try de city one more time. Maybe-so dis time be alright. De last time be not so good. Maybe-so ol' John get de chance ta show dat de black man, he be good man, jes like de white man be."

George had no answer to combat John's hopes. The man was already well accepted on the ranches and by the cowboys. If he wanted to make a point with the people of Calgary, who was he to try to stop him? As he watched John ride off, he thought, *It looks as if the man has forgotten about his*

145

homestead too. He's searching for something. I hope he finds it. John naively entered the I. G. Baker store in Calgary in response to an advertisement for a staff position that was propped up in the window. Hoping that the remembrance of the hanging of Jesse Williams, the only black man in Calgary at that time, was fading from the collective memories of Calgarians, he stepped up to the counter and said, "Fella out der tell me dat sign in de window say you look'n fer de worker in de store."

The flustered young man behind the counter didn't have a ready reply. He tried to remember if he had ever seen a black man before. He was sure he hadn't. Somehow, even in the small prairie town, he had never crossed paths with the man who had been hung. And for certain, he had never spoken with a black man.

Instead of thinking up a response to John's question, the flustered clerk called into the back room for the store manager. When he had relayed John's message to his boss, the manager walked out of the storeroom, glanced at the clerk, and then glared at John with a look that was impossible to misunderstand. With sinking heart John swung his weight onto one foot, and then the other.

Finally, the manager said, "What is your

name please?"

"I be John, Boss."

"Well, John. If I understand what you told the clerk, you had a man on the sidewalk read our sign to you. Is that correct?"

"Yass'r, dat what happen."

"May I assume, John, that you cannot read?"

"Not so good wit de letters, Boss. Be good wit de numbers though."

"Yes, I understand. But we can't have staff in the store that don't read and write. You would have to be able to read prices and directions and write up the billings. In any case, I'm not sure having you here would be good for either you or the Baker Company. The best I can offer is a job loading and unloading freight wagons. If that would suit you, the job is available immediately."

John had given no thought to the need to read and write in order to work in a store. That he missed that obvious fact embarrassed him. But the underlying rejection, based obviously on looks and skin color, made him angry. But with a sense of sadness and resignation, he accepted the freight handling job.

After several hours work at the freight yard, the manager walked out to check on John's progress. He stood mutely while he studied the empty wagons and the carefully stacked freight. He watched John's meticulous handling of the boxes and sacks that were being loaded onto another wagon for delivery to a trading post out in the foothills. Understanding that he was looking at a man who knew how to work and to do a proper job of it, he said, "If you could read as well as you work, John, there would be little you couldn't do in this life. I'm hoping you'll stay with us for a while. I'd set you to delivering this load if you are comfortable driving a team of mules."

"Mules be no problem, Boss. Oxen and horses be no problem too."

"We'll talk about it tomorrow, John, after the wagons are all loaded."

But before that time came, life for John had changed again.

"You, there. Yes, I mean you."

The voice of authority was meant to gain attention.

John straightened his back, from where he had been leaning over the wagon, adjusting the load. Approaching him with a determined look, was a NWMP officer in full uniform.

"You want'n me, Boss?"

"I don't see anyone else out here, do you?"

148

John chose not to answer the meaningless question.

"I'm told you rode into town on a horse. Where did you get the animal and where is he now?"

Befuddled at the line of enquiry, John stumbled an answer, which caused the officer even more suspicion than he had when he walked into the freight yard.

Finally, John was able to say, "Dat be my own horse, Boss. Bought him off de Bar U ranch long time ago. He be here in de barn."

The officer walked into the barn to see for himself. When John started to follow, the officer motioned him back.

"You stay where you are."

It didn't take long for the officer to return with a question. "That horse has two brands, the Bar U, which is a well-known and respected ranch, and then with the four nines. How do you explain that?"

"Dat be easy, Boss. Lac I toll you, de horse be bought from de Bar U when I's be work'n der. De four nines be my own brand. Brand for de horse and for de cattle too."

"Are you saying you own cattle?"

"Yassir, Boss. Dat what I be say'n. Own maybe close to one hundred head."

"And where are these animals now?"

"Dey be out on de grass jes lak all de rest

a de cattle. Be runn'n wit de John Quirk bunch. De Quirks, dey be friends o' mine."

The officer took a hard look at John before saying, "We've had some horse theft here in town. I'll be back. If I should find that you're the thief, it will be an unhappy day for you."

Without another word, the officer turned and walked away. When John looked back towards the store's loading dock, the manager was standing there. How long he had been watching John didn't know.

"I'm sorry about that, John. This town has some growing and maturing to do. With that murder and then the hanging of the black man, some months ago, hard feelings have taken a firm hold on people. You're paying a price for that before anyone even gets to know you. But I still say you're a good worker and I have no reason to think you're not honest. I'll still put you on as a driver if you're up to it."

"I's thank'n you fo' dat, Boss, but I'm think'n de best place fo ol' John is back on de grass. De ranchers, dey know dat I be good wit de horses an de cattle. I finish dis load fo' you, den I ride back to De Cross'n."

John's lonely ride back south gave him time for contemplation. There was still something inside that he couldn't clearly

150

explain, even to himself. Something that was pushing him to demand acceptance by the people of Calgary. But he had no clear idea how to find or take advantage of that acceptance. And as he admitted to himself, it made no logical sense. He knew he was well respected, even, perhaps loved by some, here on the grass. He was secretly proud of his belief that he could seek employment on any ranch in Alberta and immediately be put on the payroll. Wasn't that enough?

He didn't answer the silent question until his horse had taken many more steps on his southward journey. Finally, he spoke to his horse.

"Horse, you and me, we go again, come by'n'by, to da big city what isn't as big as mos' folks up der think it be. We go agin an' we show dem folks that ol' John jest as good as dey be."

With that decided in the silence of his mind, and then explained to the horse, he rode to the new ranch that was still in the building process, out on the banks of Sheep Creek. A man named Barter was managing the place. For some reason that eluded John, and most others in the district, the ranch had been named The Quorn.

CHAPTER 16

John J. Barter, manager of the newly established Quorn ranch, was saddling a black gelding in the smaller of the three corrals when John rode up, stopping within easy talking distance. Barter had seen him coming. When he heard the hoof falls come to a stop close by, he raised his head to look over the saddle.

"Morning, John. It's a bright and beautiful day, is it not?"

"Yassir, it be a fine day de Lord has given us."

"I heard you went up to the big city. What's happening up there, John? Did you find the work you were hoping for?"

"No Boss. Jest de work unloading de freight from de wagons. That not be de work I be want'n."

The two men waited silently, each thinking his own thoughts as Barter completed the adjustments on the saddle. With that done, he dropped the stirrup and fender into place, gave a firm tug on the saddle horn to assure its stability and then looked back over at John.

After figuring out that John wasn't going to come right out and ask for a job and being aware that the black man would be a great asset on the Quorn, he said, "There's a sight of building going to happen here, John. Bunk house and kitchen are up now and ready for use. The first barn is started. There will be other barns, as well, all in good time. By spring, the big house will be up and furnished, if the winter weather doesn't stop the men from working.

"We're bringing in some blooded stallions in the early spring. We will want them to get acclimatized, but until they are, they will be kept in the barn. We'll take them out each day and exercise them. Besides feeding them in the barn, we'll let them learn to scratch through whatever snow is still around for their feed.

"Tom Lynch will be heading to Montana, or perhaps further afield, looking for top grade mares and a few geldings. We'll breed the mares back to the blooded thoroughbreds. We can use a few more geldings for the working remuda. The Quorn plans to have the best riding stock on Alberta grass.

"When full spring rolls around again there will be several gents and ladies riding the steam ships across the Atlantic and then the CPR to Calgary. They are all friends of the British owners. They will be our guests here on the Quorn. I'll want the horses in tip top condition for when they arrive. They'll want to be riding to the hounds, as they call it, hunting foxes, you know. Well, we can't gather up any foxes and our hounds are few in number but there's coyotes a-plenty and miles of grass to chase them across.

"The thing is, John; the working remuda we now have will need to be cared for through the winter and be ready for hard riding in the spring, when our cattle arrive. Can you see yourself taking on that job?"

"Yassir, Boss. I be happy ta stay here."

"Well, you get yourself over to the bunk-house. There's lots of bunks. Claim which-ever one you want and settle in."

In some ways it was the easiest winter John had spent on the prairies. But then would come a bitterly cold morning, the sun bright, with frost crystals hanging in the air. And John would earn his keep.

The few other cowboys on the Quorn had brought the riding stock up to the corrals for John's care. Some of these geldings had seen little use and were perfectly content to keep it that way. But a horse that won't behave on the range was a detriment and a potential hazard, to both the rider and the other stock. John was determined to take the 'wild' out of each one before the cattle herd arrived in the spring.

Swinging a heavy stock saddle onto the rigid back of a reluctant gelding on a cold morning was a test of man and animal, both. A saddle that felt reassuringly firm in the warmth of summer was like a block of granite when the temperature dipped below zero, with the wind whipping the snow around the corners of the buildings. When John stepped aboard an animal that lived in those conditions, he might find himself enjoying a relatively peaceful ride or he might have tied onto a whirlwind of anger and hate and fear. But whatever happened, John would stick to his purpose. Only rarely did he have to pick himself up from the snow and climb aboard again.

By spring he knew each horse by both name and inclinations. Most became gentled into dependable work horses without taking all the spirit out of them. A few still liked to test their rider. An early morning bucking contest set both horse and rider up for the day, before settling down to work.

155

John corralled three horses by themselves, telling Barter that they should either be shot or driven off into the hills or sold to the Blackfoot, who seemed to have an insatiable desire for more and more horses. Having given up on the beasts, John thought of them no more.

It was a bright and welcoming day in early spring when the thoroughbred stallions arrived at the Calgary CPR corrals. John and several other Quorn riders had travelled up to unload them and drive them to the ranch.

John took a long look before declaring, "Dey be de finest horses Ol' John ever be see'n. Blandon, down to da Double X ranch by Fort Worth, he kept what he call his runners. I be work'n wit them runners all one winter. Dey be sure enough fast. Look mostly like des here thoroughbreds. Good horses on dat Blandon ranch. But I'm think'n dey be not so good as des here. We's gett'n good foals from des stallions and de tough range mares. Best we git des down ta the ranch where dey be safe."

Along with the horses came a group of hunting hounds. They were driven to the Quorn along with the stallions. The dogs didn't appear to be too bright, being unruly and causing endless problems before the crew managed to get them out of Calgary and into the open country. Even in the open the fool dogs were forever getting in the way of horse and rider and threatening to run off in all directions in the open grasslands, John fell in love with them anyway.

"Dey be young still. Dey be learn'n pretty soon, I'm tink'n," was his excuse for their erratic behavior.

Not long after the arrival of the stallions, Tom Lynch rode in with his herd of Montana mares, most of them ready to drop a foal in the next few weeks. Along with the mares came a good selection of working geldings.

The additional horses were turned over to John's care. It would be his job to have the geldings ready for the demands the larger cattle herd would place on horses and riders both, when it arrived.

John's workload was increasing. Foals were being born, and, when the time was right, the new stallions were put into service with the Montana mares. With the breaking and gentling of the new geldings, on top of getting to know the dogs and their mannerisms, John found himself with little free time, but still as contented as he had ever been.

He thought of his abandoned homestead plot from time to time but didn't go near it again. The last time he had ridden past, it appeared that someone had salvaged about one half of his cut and trimmed logs.

In the back of his mind, John was still burdened by his failure to find acceptance in Calgary. But that happy day would have to come on a later occasion. There was no time for a trip to the city now. The Quorn was expecting their British visitors.

John had been warned that riding and hunting would be high on the list of desires the visiting men would have.

As it turned out, more than one group of visitors came that summer. They came with their high-born attitudes of privilege and self-righteousness. And they came with their British flat saddles, a device that John judged as being foolish and totally hopeless so far as a working saddle was concerned. It wasn't until after some unfortunate experiences during the coyotes chases, and even more unfortunate experiences with the firmness of prairie sod, as one rider after another found to their dismay, that John finally convinced the men to try a western, working saddle.

For the most part, John not only won the men over to the western saddles, but he won them over to himself. One by one, the lords and counts and earls, men who barely talked to those beneath their stations in life at home, came to respect the black horseman.

Men who arrived for a visit on the Alberta prairies with rigid beliefs in their own rightness and superiority, as often as not, boarded the CPR in Calgary, for their return trip to England, with adjusted ideas and much to think about, if their captured minds would allow such thinking.

CHAPTER 17

George Lane walked into the general merchandise store at High River and spotted John. After shaking hands in a warm greeting the two men walked together into the spring sunshine. There was always time for a visit between men who lived and worked miles apart and where visits could have many months between them. A bit of time with a neighbor was not considered to be wasted time.

"How was your winter on the Quorn, John? You look as fit as ever. Did your stock come through all right?"

"Stock be do'n jest fine, George. Winter not be so hard as before. We's plann'n fo putt'n up lots a hay too. I'm think'n we's all should be putt'n up de hay. Lots of work, but better dan hav'n dead cows, come de springtime."

"You're right on that, my friend. I have no idea how many tons of hay the Bar U put up last fall, but it was a lot. I'm sure some ranchers will continue taking their chances but our losses over the few years of ranching here have been too high. We can't justify those losses. It's not fair to the animals, either. I can't imagine their suffering in some of these winter storms where they can find no shelter, nor feed or water.

"There are a lot of other changes taking place on this grass too. Cattle prices have fallen, while the value of good horses continues to rise. There seems to be an unlimited demand for good working stock, both riding and heavy animals. Some fellas have gone out of cattle and totally into horses."

While John loved horses, especially the Quorn horses that he had babied through their first Alberta winter, and the grey mare John Barter had given to him, he still found himself thinking of cattle when the bunk-house talk got around to considering the future. His own little herd had suffered loss but was slowly re-gaining ground and he hoped, would soon be back up to the numbers that had carried his brand just a short two years before. In any case, he continued to save every penny he earned, towards the purchase of more breeding cows. He never talked about it, but he had brought a small cache of gold coins with him on his long ride to the north. Ever a saver and only reluctantly a spender, John still had a part of the wages earned on the MacIntyre Horse Farm. And the sale price of the livery business had remained untouched. These savings would be put to good use when he had a spread of his own and would be able to care for the cattle. He had little faith in allowing animals to run loose, breeding to the first scrub bull that wandered their way and suffering the long cold winters without help. No, John figured to take good care of his animals when the time came.

"Ah've ridden dis grass from the south border right up ta Calgary. Dat be a lot of grass. Maybe-so be too much for jes de horses. I don' know what de country do wit' so many horses."

George chuckled and said, "Well, you're right on that, John. It's a powerful lot of grass. But the entire west is open for home-steading, one quarter section at a time. That's thousands of farms being established in a very short space of time. There's a lot of country suitable for farming or ranching to the north of Calgary. Hundreds of miles to the north. And from the foothills to the far eastern lake country. One quarter sec-tion to a man, or sometimes, two quarters for a family. Much of that land is covered in light forest or bush. And every one of those families will need riding animals as well as heavies for the clearing of land, plus the pulling of machinery and wagons.

"But, still, I hope you're proven to be correct. Once a farmer buys a horse, he's good for many years, whereas everyone has to eat regularly. That means beef. We'll keep offering the very best beef on the market from the Bar U. We'll be sorting them out during the fall roundup, John. We should have several hundred fat steers to offer to the market."

John was quiet as he thought back over the few years there had been cattle on Alberta grass. He mentioned his wonder at the growth in both ranches and numbers of cattle to George.

"You are absolutely correct again, John. You weren't among the very first to arrive here, but you weren't far behind. You were here before me. You've seen the ranching business grow and expand faster than anyone ever thought possible. That so much could happen in so few years is a thing of wonder. Not much more than five years after the first small start, there are over a hundred thousand head on grass, by some estimates."

The two men visited for another few minutes before they shook and went their separate ways.

Tom Lynch had completed what was to be his last drive. This time, instead of cattle he had gone to Oregon after quality breeding horses, including a big bunch for his own ranch. Over the past couple of years many ranches had been taken over by new owners. A few of the original settlers had been driven into insolvency by winter losses, with the drop in cattle prices making it impossible to recover with the few animals they had left.

Other owners had succumbed to the temptation represented by the cash offers presented to them by the big British and Eastern investors. George Emerson and Tom Lynch, long time partners in a variety of enterprises had gone their separate ways, with George having become almost totally immersed in the building up of High River, the new town beside the Highwood, where The Crossing and Smith and French had held the ground for so long.

As ranchers worldwide were apt to do, men from far and near rode to Lynch's new ranch holdings, on hearing the news of his return, intent on viewing his large herd of breeding mares driven in from down south. John and his boss on the Quorn, John Barter rode over together.

With men from so many ranches gathering in one place, the talk was of horses and cattle, to the exclusion of most other topics. With a question from one of the men, Tom Lynch held the group's attention while he said, "Well now, boys. You're wondering how the last drive went. And it's a fair enough question, what with all the changes across the land, both here in Alberta as well as to the south in Montana and other states.

"The truth is that this was my last drive. It's an activity I always enjoyed. Met a lot of good folks and saw a lot of the beauty of God's creation. But the unmistakable fact is that the land is growing up and closing in. From Oregon, which, by the way, is a powerful long way from The Crossing, we ran into settled farms and ranches, and enough barb wire to discourage all you open range ranchers if I should tell of it all. The drive took far longer than it would have five years ago, or even two years ago.

"Everywhere we rode, the homesteaders were taking up land that the big ranchers had used and treated as their own for many years. A lot of good grass has been turned under in the hopes of growing a wheat crop or whatever the settler had in mind.

"That's real tough on the ranchers but it's legal and the law is on the side of the homesteaders. It's the same here in Alberta. In fact, the rumor around is that the twenty-one-year leases will not be renewed when their term expires. Now, that's still a long while into the future and much can change before then, but the threat is there, nonetheless. Hard to think of a rancher investing money and years of work building up a brand, only to lose it with the stroke of a government pen. The government wants taxpayers and voters. A single large, leased ranch can be divided into hundreds of homesteads. That most of them will fail within two or three years in this dry, windy country doesn't seem to interest the government boys. But the homesteaders will plow up this wonderful native grass and then move on, leaving the country poorer for their coming.

"But, hey, you're here to see the new mares and talk of brighter things. And I've got a horse I want you to see. He'll never be a ranch horse or ridden to church by your maiden aunt. But buck? Why, I want to tell you! I've seen some buckers over the years, or I thought I had. But this big fella takes the idea to a whole other place. Come

166

down here to the corral and take a look at him."

The men gathered around the outside of the poplar pole fencing and studied the outlaw brute. Someone shouted out, "Looks pretty ordinary to me, just a-standing there, Tom. You sure you got the right horse?"

That brought good natured chuckling from the men until someone hollered out, "Well, I'll put up the first five dollars towards a kitty to cover the medical expenses of the first man to sit his saddle."

"I've another five over here."

"Add mine to it too."

And so, the jesting went, until another rancher said, "Who have you got to ride him, Tom? You going to do it yourself?"

Tom laughed and answered, "I wouldn't get on that brute if you threw in your entire ranch. No not me. Young fella here though. Just up from Montana. Did some riding, or so it's been told. How about it, Frank?"

The man being addressed spit out the grass stem he had been chewing on and took a careful look at the outlaw horse. As he was hesitating, George Stimson, filled with local pride, and thinking that if anyone rode him it shouldn't be a newcomer that no one knew, said, "I'm thinking if anyone can ride that animal it would be John Ware.

How about it, John?"

John, always ready for a jest or a laugh or for making an extra dollar or two, answered, "All dat money you fellas be put'n up, dat be enough fo Ol' John ta buy me another cow fo' ta add ta my bunch. Shure, I ride dat horse. He don' look so mean ta me."

Frank, the young rider just up from Montana took a sideways glance at John, wondering if the black man knew what he was getting in for. He had seen the clear marks of an outlaw horse in his first look at the animal.

John never made an issue of his knowledge of horses. He had, nonetheless, seen the same trend marks on the one in the corral. But he took it as a challenge. And as the opportunity to earn one more cow for his long-awaited ranch.

Three of Tom's riders, working together, managed to get the saddle and bridle on the outlaw, in a whinnying, stomping, dust raising few minutes, with one cowboy getting foot stomped in the process.

Tom hollered, "Bring him out here fellas. One of you keep a firm hold to that bridle while John gets his seat."

John looked the outlaw up and down as he walked around him before mounting. He spoke, as if the horse could understand and

168

just might answer.

"Is you'se sech a bad one? Don't look so bad. That one eye's a bit slanted and fearsome look'n but I'm think'n you don't mean noth'n by it. How about you and I jest go fo' a bit of a trot around dis here pasture, jest like we was goin' on a picnic wit de pretty lady."

As he talked, John took the reins from the cowboy standing by and continued to walk along the horse's flank. Stroking the animal's neck and back and side, John talked the whole time. He gave a pull on the horn to assure himself that the saddle was well settled and continued to talk and stroke the grey-haired hide. As he stroked, the horse flinched and twitched his hide as if he was shaking off a pestering fly. John continued to talk.

Someone in the crowd hollered out, "You going to sing him to sleep now, John?"

As the watchers were laughing at the remark John, defying gravity, gripped the horn with his left hand, the reins wound around the fingers of that hand, and with a single thrust of his powerful legs vaulted into the saddle. The horse took long enough to get over his shock to allow John to find the stirrups. Showing a bit of flare for showmanship, John removed his much-abused hat and swatted the horse on the rump.

"Show me da ride, horse."

For years after, and even in the history books of southern Alberta, what ensued in the two minutes after John landed in the saddle of the grey outlaw, was a story of constant interest. Men who were there in person told of it to their children and grandchildren. Historians would seek out the last surviving eyewitnesses. When the tale seemed to be exaggerated, the teller would assure the listener that it was all true, that, in fact, he lacked the words to give the story its due. Invariably the story would end with something like, "that monster horse never gave up the fight and John never got thrown. Laughing and waving his hat in the air between whaps on the animal's rump, that black rider stayed in the leather until Tom Lynch hollered, 'That's enough John. You've proved your merit, you and the horse both. Leave some anger for the next man to try him'."

Slipping his feet from the stirrups, John swung his right leg over the neck of the horse and dropped to the grass, laughing the whole while. With infinite timing, he somehow managed to whap the horse one more time with his hat and avoid a driving hind hoof. Three mounted cowboys roped the fighting tornado and drove him into the corral. With the leather removed, he settled down and stared hatred at every man present.

The Montana rider looked on in wonder and shook his head at the thought that it might have been him riding that tornado.

CHAPTER 18

Summer was a busy time on the Quorn and the Bar U, and all other ranches, large or small. There were buildings to erect, fences to be built, cows and calves alike to be cared for, branding to be done and young bulls to be turned into steers for beefing.

As summer progressed, wise ranchers' eyes turned to the need for hay. The Quorn completed the purchase of a new mowing machine, plus a horse powered hay rake, relieving the need for crews of men swinging scythes. Many other ranchers had been moving in that same direction.

John was left with the care of the breeding horses, plus the riding animals and the dogs. Guests from Britain and the cities of Eastern Canada continued to arrive. A brave few brought their women with them. Some, men and women both, caused no end of problems with their pride and arrogance and their demands, while others joined in the adventure. A rare few even offered to assist John in the care of the animals he assigned for their use, pleased it seemed to get them away from their overbearing countrymen for a few minutes, at least.

But as the calendar showed September, and the weather turned towards cool mornings and late summer rains, the guests were driven to Calgary to meet the trains that would hustle them back east, where they could board the ships that would take them back to the Old Country.

For the more established ranches, the fall roundup was called. It was time to sort the heavy, saleable steers from the herd. They would be gathered and readied for the drive to the waiting CPR cattle cars, in Calgary. This would be the first large shipment of mature steers born to the original Montana cross-bred stock.

The Quorn had no mature animals to ship. At George Lane's request, John Ware was released from his duties at the Quorn in order to accompany the Bar U crew as they drove their sales animals to the rails. With some reluctance, remembering his previous visits to the big city, John saddled up and rode along with the crew.

The drive was short, only a few days. With steers and riders alike mastering their first attempt at loading railcars, the animals were soon on their long journey to England, and to what George Lane hoped was a better market than what producers faced in Eastern Canada.

In spite of some rude treatment by the small-minded town police force, John rode home with a brighter feeling towards the people of Calgary. The chances of him visiting again increased considerably.

Shortly after his return to the Quorn, John was approached by his friend Sam Howe.

"Barter has given us both the time we need to search out the land to the west, John. Grab your gear and saddle up. We've talked enough about this. It's time we found our futures, and those futures aren't in working for thirty dollars a month and our keep. Our futures are in having land and cattle for ourselves. I'm thinking that country further to the west, the foothills country, needs another long look."

"I been der when hunt'n fer de gold wit Dan Riley an ol' French. Dat sure be a pretty 'nuff country. Big ranchers not be usn'n most of dat land yet. Joe Davis and de Quirks, dey be out der now. My own four nines are out there with the Quirks bunch, so maybe-so dey be at der new home before ol' John be der himself. Maybe-so we find de good places."

The two men rode west, enjoying the bracing freshness of the early fall mornings, driven forward by the idea of land and freedom, or at least, self-reliance, for themselves. Over the years both men had experienced the bitterness of a hard winter and the disaster befalling the unprepared ranches. They were determined that wherever they settled, they would do everything possible so that men and animals alike, would be prepared for whatever the climate threw at them.

After several days of riding the foothill country, they came to some solid conclusions. These were expressed by Sam.

"It's a wonderful country, John. Close to the mountains like it is, there could well be more snow, although the forests may provide the shelters the cattle need. It's possible too that the winds will be less than they are on the open grasslands. We won't know any of that until we've lived there awhile. And these forests will supply the logs for building, and an endless source of firewood, too."

John agreed and then added, "Shor' 'nuff have to put up de hay out here."

Looking around as he rode, he again said, "My, my, it shor' do be a pretty country."

John reveled in the spread of well-watered, empty land before him. As much as he loved the wide-open prairie with its miles upon miles of waving grass, he found these foothills much to his liking. And really, he was only a few miles from that much loved open grassland.

At his earlier, abandoned homestead claim, down by The Crossing he had to cut logs for building, gathering them from the scarce growth along the Highwood, a considerable distance from where he planned to establish Ware Ranch. Dragging the heavy timber that distance and knowing that year by year his firewood would have to be dragged the same distance had discouraged him.

Most of the newer ranch buildings going up were built from cut lumber, hauled by wagon from distant mills. For John to follow suit would needlessly drain his pockets of his precious cattle-buying savings. No, he needed logs that could be cut and peeled and turned into a perfectly acceptable dwelling, purchased with the sweat of his brow alone. As he rode through and studied the close-by foothills, he saw a wealth of trees, lodgepole pine and spruce mostly. Being of largely the same age, they were also close in size. Those standing trees, cut and trimmed into matching logs, represented the Ware Ranch cabin, firewood, corrals and outbuildings. All built with a minimum of coins reluctantly lifted from his leather poke.

And everywhere he and Sam rode, winding among the higher up hills, and through the lower-down poplar and other deciduous trees, there was grass in abundance. Put together with the several flowing streams they had crossed during their ride, it appeared as the land of promise.

There was no telling what decision Sam would make but for John, he had found his place. Here he would measure out his quarter section and here he would stake his claim. The claimed land, along with the open grazing around him, plus whatever he would be able to purchase in future years would be his key to prosperity and happiness. Here he would build and here he would stay.

On the ride home they turned the horses towards a still pond, thinking to water both themselves and the horses. But when the horses bent to drink, they quickly pulled back and shook their heads. Wondering what the problem was, John stepped to the ground and scooped up a handful of the scummy water. Lifting it to his nose, he quickly pulled back, just as the horses had done. He dropped the water and wiped his hand on the grass and then on his pant leg.

Turning up to the still mounted Sam he said, "Shore 'nuff be someth'n in dis water. Cain't drink noth'n like dis. Stink lak some kind of oil."

Rubbing his still scummy, slippery fingers together, he looked at them and again spoke to Sam. "Be slippery, jest lak de greese we us'n fo de wagon wheels. Where dat oil be com'n from?"

Sam reached into a saddle bag and withdrew a small glass jar with a lid. He dumped the small bit of remaining cooking salt from it and said, "Here, John, dip up some of that oily water. We'll take it back with us."

"How we be tell'n folks where we gitt'n dis oily water, Sam?"

Sam considered the question for a moment before answering, "Well, we know we're in Sheep Creek country and we know that a fella named John Turner settled close by here a couple of years ago, although I've never met him or been to his place. We could tell John Barter that much and let the big boys figure it out from there. If they're even interested, that is. Of course, we could bring someone out here, show them the way, if push came to shove.

"For my part, I'm only interested in the grass. Let someone else figure out where the oil came from. Unless, of course, we could dip some up for lighting our lanterns, but I don't suppose that's going to happen."

And so, the men turned their horses back to the Quorn ranch, putting the future Turner Valley oil fields behind them without a further thought.

The days of the longhorn running loose on Alberta grass hadn't lasted more than a couple of years. It now existed only in memory, although their mixed breed progeny was still there in abundance. Also, long past was the big Eastern market's willingness to suffer through the stringy beef that hung on the longhorns' bones. While the longhorn and their mixed breed offspring were tough, tolerating range conditions that would prove detrimental to more refined breeds, the unpleasant truth was that they were simply not wanted by the beef marketers.

The ranches were importing refined, quality beef animals for breeding, from Eastern Canada, as well as Britain and Europe. Breeds a lot of western cattlemen had never heard of before. Fear of having an expensive imported cow bred back to a wild range bull

179

was a continuing challenge to the hard-working ranchers. Riders were detailed off to circle the herds, driving the determined bulls back. It was a hopeless task. The country was too big, the cattle too spread out, the nights too dark to follow, or see where the animals were going, the riders too few. To complicate matters, the cows didn't seem to have any preference as to what daddy their calves would claim.

The two most obvious answers to the dilemma were to string miles of barb wire or eliminate the range bulls. Since most ranchers were, at heart, open range men, the remaining option was obvious. It wasn't talked about a lot, but each rider carried a carbine with him. Slowly, over time, the problem would be dealt with.

There was considerable competition among strong minded men as to which heavy breed was most suited to the prairie grass and conditions, and which produced the most beef per animal. Although many breeds had their supporters as well as their good points, it was the Hereford and the Angus, both black and red, that won the day.

John looked on as all of this was transpiring, knowing that his little band of cross cows and calves could not measure up to the new animals appearing on the wealthy ranches. He also knew the obvious truth; his cache of saved coins was not going to purchase many top-quality cows, or even a single bull.

"Someday I have de best as what anyone have. Jest fer now I keep dis what I already got."

John, ever showing his willingness to change and move, left the Quorn and his beloved horses and dogs, and took up a place on the High River Horse Ranch. The job included an increase in wages as well as the opportunity to work with some of the best horses ever imported into the country. But the final attraction was the bit of extra time off to work with his own small herd. He longed to give them the care they deserved and needed; anything that would move him closer to that dreamed-of ranch on an as-yet unchosen foothills creek.

CHAPTER 19

On a quarter section homestead at the little settlement of Shephard, just south of Calgary, the Dan Lewis family had recently arrived from Toronto and settled in. The family consisted of Dan, his wife and four children. Mildred was their eldest, and by pioneer standards, was considered to be of marriageable age.

There were more black families in the Ontario region of the nation, but few had yet to arrive in the west. Some of these folks had entered the new land of freedom, years before, on the underground railway, the multifaceted route that smuggled escaped slaves from the south, through many miles of harrowing experiences and constant dangers, and with the assistance of many brave volunteers.

The Lewis family was not of that background. They were a free people, quite possibly having slavery somewhere in the dark, dim family past, conceivably in Nova Scotia when that area was under British rule, but they themselves had never known slavery. Nor had slavery ever been legal or acceptable in Canada. The slavery in Nova Scotia had been abandoned when it was made illegal in 1833 by an act of the British parliament, well before Canada became an independent nation in 1867.

The people of Calgary were slowly putting the murder of James Adams and the hanging of the black man, Jesse Williams behind them. John had found his visits to the city to be slowly improving and the Lewis family was accepted, at least to the point where they were able to sell their little bit of farm produce into the Calgary fresh food market, at the I. G. Baker store.

When John Barton returned from the city with news of having met the Lewis family, with their nineteen-year-old daughter, Mildred, he was quick to extend this information to John. Of course, such news is not easily contained, and in the tight quarters of a bunk house there is no chance at all of secrecy. John was soon the recipient of considerable teasing.

Duncan McPherson, John's new employer at the High River Horse Ranch schemed a way to have John at a location where he might meet the Lewis family. John Barton had passed along the information that the Lewises were in the habit of making Thursdays their shopping day in the big city.

"John, I have a bit of business that needs to be done in Calgary and you're the man for the job. I've placed orders to be filled and ready for pickup on Thursday afternoon this week. The biggest order will be at the Baker store, but there will be a couple of others. I'll clear that up for you before you go. They'll be some weight to carry so I'll be wanting you to take the democrat buggy and a solid team. You'll have to leave on Wednesday morning and be prepared to camp out the one night.

"There's just a chance that you may meet these new folks we're hearing about. That's all up to you. You'll have to figure it out for yourself. My only advice would be to have a bath and put on clean clothing. Carry a change of clothing with you in case you fall in the river or meet up with some other calamity.

"We're all wishing you good fortune on this, John, in spite of the teasing. We're hoping you can make some good friends of this new family."

CHAPTER 20

As more and more women arrived in the west, some of them the wives of those men already there, others, ladies who had answered inquiring advertisements in Eastern papers, or were somehow introduced to one of the many lonely men in Alberta, John's mind went also in that direction.

He seldom talked about the matter, but the obvious truth was that he had a great yearning for a wife and family. On the trip to the Sheep Creek country with Sam Howe, he spoke of this closely held desire just the one time. It happened at the end of a long day of riding, as the fire was burning low, and the last cups of coffee had emptied the pot. For when is a man most likely to reveal his heart, as if he was talking only to himself, with not another man anywhere around? The warm summer evening with the darkness folding itself around the slowly dying fire, and the hint of melancholy easing its way into the minds of men too long alone, men without female companionship for months and years at a time, only added to the sharing of secrets.

"Sam, I'm think when I die someone take my horse and saddle. Take my dog and de cows. Someone else maybe-so live'n in my house. But no one ever remember ol' black John Ware.

"Most men, dey leav'n de family behind dem. Maybe-so a son what will carry de name.

"It be good if'n der be someone left dat remember ol' John. Maybe-so, one of dem picture tak'n fellas, dey be tak'n de picture, and de son, he be keep'n dat picture. He be say'n, 'dis black man you see here, he be my father. He be'n de slave. Now you see what he be build'n. Got de ranch and de cows and dis family. Dat my father, right der. He no be'n slave no more.' "

Sam listened and somehow felt John's aloneness and his loneliness, and the lifetime of hurts hidden under the simple words. Silently he wondered at the subtle difference between being alone and being lonely.

Both men drank from their heavy crockery mugs as they looked at each other across the small fire.

"You and I, John, we both need wives."

"Where at dis ol' black fella, he be find'n colored lady what will live wit' him? She look at ol' John, she say, 'dat man, he cain't neither read nor write. He cain't speak de language so good. Cain't somehow say de words proper. He be an ignorant man, dat John. An' he be gett'n old.' What colored lady der be fo me?"

"I don't know, John. I can't answer your questions. But you've been known to say that you believe God will look after us. It could be that God has a lady somewhere just for you."

John studied his riding mate as if his words had put a new, and yet old slant on the conversation.

"Maybe-so dat be true. Maybe-so, come by n by."

CHAPTER 21

On this beautiful day in early May, the well-trod wagon trail to Calgary was no challenge to John or the wagon team. The hills were slight, more rolling prairie than true hills. That would remain the case until the river valleys of the Bow and Elbow were encountered just a few miles to the north. The horses needed little guidance as they followed the two-track trail north. John, leaning back on the wagon seat, the reins slack in his hand and with his faithful dog sitting upright on the seat beside him, as if he too were enjoying the warm morning, studied the land.

The trees were losing their winter's gray, bleak look and taking on the fresh, welcome green of spring. The summer's more mature, more dusky green would soon replace the brilliance and newness of the just sprouting leaves and grasses. The yellows and golds of the last fall's fallen poplar and aspen leaves made a carpet in the forest and brush lands. And the red bark of the willows along the small watercourses had taken on new life.

John well knew that the Alberta weather was unpredictable at any time, but spring and fall could hold the most surprises. A sunny day could cloud up and drop a shower or a torrent with little notice.

With a drop in temperature, an early fall shower could turn to a rain and snow mixture and then to a slushy snow and, if the temperature continued to drop, to an all-out early snowfall; the wet, heavy snow that gathered on the leaves and bent tree limbs to the ground and froze out whatever was left unpicked in the vegetable gardens.

John well knew from experience that the same surprise could visit itself upon the land in late spring. Nothing could be taken for granted with Alberta weather.

The captivating beauty of the close-by snowcapped Rockies held a warning that aware and knowledgeable people were ever watching for. A wind dropping across those sky-high glaciers could turn a warm day into a prelude of the winter to come, or a warning that winter was not truly past and could reappear in just a matter of minutes, or at most, hours.

At that time, the rancher needed to have

189

his hay in stacks, his log buildings well chinked and his needed supplies on hand. The rider or wagon master would want to unwrap his bedroll and turn out his yellow rain slicker or, perhaps, his sheep skin coat. Riding in constantly windy country, he might want to drop the chin strap on his Stetson into place.

But on this day, on this trail, the weather treated the country, and the traveler, kindly. As always, there was the need for one night's layover, giving rest to the team and to John. The dog, who had done nothing all day but sit on the wagon seat, was bounding with energy. A small, close by hillside, riddled with gophers, kept the animal busy. He had little chance of catching one of the wily animals who would tease and chatter and then, at the last second, turn, flip his tail, and scamper into the safety of his tunnel, leaving the excited but distraught dog yapping and turning in circles while he sought out another potential victim.

John arrived in Calgary near noon the second day. With a plan to arrive at the I. G. Baker store around midafternoon, he made his other pickups first, and then drove down to the edge of the Bow River where he staked the team on good grass and fed the dog some leftovers brought from the ranch kitchen. He then washed his hands in the river, took a refreshing drink himself and leaned against a wagon wheel while he ate the last of the sandwiches prepared for him by the cook.

Pulling the wagon into the shade at the big loading dock behind the Baker trading post, he tied the team, told the dog to stay, and entered the store through the warehouse. After greeting a familiar clerk and explaining about the wagon being ready for loading, he entered the store itself. The first person he saw, fingering the leather of a fancy, brass studded driving harness, was John Barter.

As he fingered the harness, Barter was visiting with a large black man. Seeing John enter the store, he waved and called out, across the rows and stacks of shirts, work pants, boots, and mounds of anything a working cattleman or farmer might need.

"John, good to see you. Come over here. There's someone I want you to meet."

Dan Lewis turned to follow Barter's eyes. His own eyes lit up at the sight of another black man coming his way. The two strangers locked eyes and stared, as the space between them shrank. When they were within hand shaking distance Barter said, "Dan Lewis, I want you to meet a good friend of mine. This is John Ware. John was one of the first to drive a herd into the area. Been out here on the grasslands for some years now, making a name for himself as a cattleman, horseman and all-around trustworthy friend. He's a good man to know.

"John, Dan and his family have only been in the area for a few months, but they're already established on their own piece of land just to the south a few miles."

The two black men shook hands while they studied each other, as if everything they needed to know could be seen through their eyes or felt in the handshake.

John's heart seemed as if it might burst through his ribs and flop, bleeding but happy, onto the I. G. Baker floor. How long had it been since he had taken fellowship with another colored man? Months? Most likely it was years. The few coloreds whose paths he had crossed since leaving Texas were simply a shadow that drifted across his life, never lingering for more than a few days or weeks, at most. No one had ever stayed long enough to establish a friendship of any sort. But here was a man who had brought his family to a new land and was settling down. Here was an opportunity worthy of his attention. That there was, apparently, a daughter of marriageable age was another matter to be thoroughly explored.

"I's pleased to meet you, Dan. De ranch be some miles from here, but on dis grass-land a few miles don' mean much when folks be long'n to have a visit. I shur be pleased to get to know y'all come by n by."

"Thank you, John. We would be pleased to get to know you as well. We're still trying to get used to the distances here in the west ourselves. It sometimes seems as if there can't be any more distance or any more grass or any more mountains, and then we top a hill and there, ahead of us is more of everything. It's a beautiful country though and we're looking forward to getting our farm built up and getting ourselves properly settled in.

"Perhaps you could come for a visit one Sunday afternoon soon. I know the family would like to get to know you too. In fact, there they are now, just coming into the store. Come, I'll introduce you."

As Dan turned to lead the way, the two Johns, Barter and Ware glanced at each other, with Barter grinning just a bit while he nodded for John Ware to follow along. The family: wife and three children had stopped just inside the store doorway, their eyes fixed on this black man that was being led their way. It required only a few steps to cross the floor to where the family was standing, waiting.

Dan Lewis half turned towards John and said, "John, I'd like you to say hello to Mrs. Lewis. And these are our three youngest children."

Mrs. Lewis waited while her husband spoke the kid's names before she added, "We have another girl. Mildred is her name. She'll be along shortly."

As excited as John was to meet the Lewis family, especially nineteen-year-old Mildred, who arrived just moments after her mother first spoke of her, he was conscious of the fact that the day was more advanced than he had first planned on. There was still work that needed doing back at the ranch. And the cookhouse would be waiting for the supplies being packed into the back of the wagon.

The trail that would return John to the ranch with the loaded wagon, would not be shortened with the excitement of having met the Lewises. John had to get back onto that trail, and he knew the Lewis family would have work of their own to do, back on their small homestead. They parted shortly, with smiles and an arrangement for John to come for dinner in a couple of weeks.

With the date, and the directions to the farm firmly held in John's head, he said his goodbyes and walked to the back of the store to help the clerk load the last of the supplies.

The first nervous visit to the Lewis home on a bright spring Sunday in 1890, had John's carefully rehearsed words replaced with ramblings interspersed with awkward silences. For all John's competence and self-assurance out on the range or sitting the saddle on a half-broke horse, or in a bunkhouse full of men, he admitted to himself that he was uncomfortable socially in mixed company. His life had consisted of the confines of slavery and the often rowdy and boisterous fellowship of the bunkhouse, with little experience in between. Despite the embarrassment about his tortured use of the language, he had gotten to where he could talk of cattle, horses and grassland conditions with men of the highest rank, from ranch owners to British peers with their snooty ways and excessive opinions of themselves. But for socializing with women, and talking of other matters, Mrs. Quirk had provided the single opportunity in his lonely life.

That good woman, the first white woman

to take up residency in the area, had silently wondered if John would welcome some lessons on reading and writing and, perhaps, elocution. Not wishing to cause unnecessary awkwardness or possibly damage their friendship, she had said nothing until, one day the topic seemed to fit easily into the conversation. When John failed to respond to her overture, she had backed off and never mentioned the thought again.

But now, with the beautiful Mildred sitting so close, in the same small room, he thought back to that day in the Quirk home. Not seeing the need at the time, and not at all sure he could sort out all the strange marks that seemed to hold such mysteries on the written page, he had turned down that good woman's offer of teaching. He now found himself embarrassed to be the only one in the house that didn't speak proper English. Or read and write.

John and Dan Lewis visited over coffee in the small farmhouse while Mrs. Lewis and Mildred fussed around putting the dinner together. As Mildred carried the dinnerware to the table, laying it on the white, carefully ironed tablecloth, she shyly raised her eyes to catch another discrete glimpse of their visitor. John wouldn't miss such a move because his eyes were seldom off the young lady, even as he carried on a conversation with her father.

Dan, somehow catching some signal that John missed, cleared his throat and said, "Well, it seems the time has come for us to move to the table. You take a seat, John, while I call in the other kids."

When everyone was seated, with John and Mildred sitting opposite each other at the same end of the table, Dan, without preamble, folded his hands and bowed his head. John, who had prayed many times, but always by himself and always silently, feared the day when someone would ask him to return thanks for the food. He was sure that would stretch his social graces to their limit. Fortunately, that hadn't happened on this first visit.

As was common with many farmwives, although she set a place for herself, the wife and cook seldom sat, spending most of her time either in the kitchen or carrying refilled food dishes between the stove and the table, and fussing over the dessert, while the family and guests ate.

An observant watcher might notice the lady taking a nibble here and a taste there, directly from the cooking pots, even as she had done throughout the preparation of the dinner. She would then declare herself to be not in the least hungry, all the time hoping, without expressing that hope in words, that it would be understood it was her duty and privilege to serve the guests.

Following the meal, many a sincere compliment arose in gratitude of the lady's hospitality and dedication, proven by her unending attendance to their needs.

On this, John's first visit to the Lewis home, Mrs. Lewis took her seat while the running and carrying was left to Mildred. While John found all the moving around to be a bit distracting, it also gave him the opportunity to lift his eyes from his plate and, at least with his peripheral vision, catch another look at the lovely young lady.

John reflected on his few opportunities to partake of a meal in a white couple's home. With just two people to come to the Quirks' table, or three when John was visiting, Mrs. Quirk was seated before Mr. Quirk lifted knife or fork. And on either the Tubbs or Blandon ranches, back in Texas, a ranch hand would be taking his life into his own hands to pick up a fork before the rancher's wife found her seat and the rancher himself gave thanks.

No matter how rough the rancher or his crew might be out on the range, in the home certain protocols of politeness were followed.

It is probable that both John and Mildred fooled themselves into thinking that no one was noticing their glances but, of course, everyone around the table was aware. At one point, when the younger brother cast a knowing glance at his father, while grinning widely, a look Mildred missed, Dan was forced to a tight-lipped grin himself.

The time and the visit went faster and better than John could have ever imagined. It also passed more quickly. And, as with all things, it had to come to an end. With his own much delayed ranch responsibilities causing an uneasy feeling in the back of his mind, he knew it was time to get back. With thanks and handshakes and several friendly, parting words, and the promise to not be a stranger, John took his leave. As he topped the small hill to the south of the Lewis home place, he pulled his horse to a stop and turned one last time, lifting his hand in a farewell wave. He smiled in gratitude and satisfaction as six arms returned his wave. He was too far away to see if there were smiles to accompany the family's waves. But he satisfied himself with the belief that the smiles were there, and genuine.

The several summer and fall visits that

followed the much remembered first one finally wound down as winter settled itself across the land. The truth was that John had to put a considerable number of miles behind him with each visit. He had, by this time, moved his cattle and his home to a property in the much-loved Sheep Creek country. The ride from his new cabin was long and trying on both man and saddle horse.

During his absences John had burdened the Quirks with the work of two ranches, their own as well as the needs on the Ware Ranch. Although those good neighbors had voiced loud assurances that John was welcome to leave as often as the urge hit him, accompanied by the reminder that a love in bloom needed personal attention, he knew the visits must end, at least until the spring snowmelt opened the land for easier travel.

Chapter 22

The distance from the new ranch on Sheep Creek to the Lewis home was long. The work on the Ware Ranch was never ending. When the spring of 1891 finally arrived, after the isolation of the long winter months, he made a quick visit. Although he was welcomed, as always, he couldn't stay long. There were newborn calves back on the Ware Ranch, calves his future depended on, or, he silently hoped, his and Mildred's futures depended on. They needed his care.

John's two hundred head of breeding cows wandered the hills and light forests adjacent to the Sheep Creek homestead. He worked long hours building corrals and caring for the stock. He knew that in late summer he would have weeks of cutting hay for winter feed. With no mechanization available to him, it was the scythe and the pitchfork, and John's enduring strength and stamina that worked together to fill the hay yard with winter cattle feed.

He had witnessed too many mistakes made by the Bar U and the Quorn and others, to risk repeating those mistakes for himself. The big ranches could afford some losses. He was not in that position.

When the winter was again upon him, he would keep his stock captured safely inside the spruce-pole fencing adjacent to his hay yard. He had no intention of allowing them to drift with the wind.

Acknowledging that he was unable to assume the risks the big ranchers took with their stock, John rode many miles during the grazing season, holding his cattle close to the home place and watching for predators.

Looking over his small herd, and grinning at the energies of the calves, his future as an independent rancher looked bright, if modest. He had no market animals to sell yet but he needed little money and he still had some savings from the few market animals he had sold from his original herd. And he still had the well protected stash of coins brought along on his trip from Texas. He would be alright until his yearlings, from the previous year's calving, were at saleable weight.

To feed himself and get his work done, John needed little that he couldn't take from the land. His cash outlay was only for some basics like coffee, sugar, salt and flour. His meat came from elk or deer taken in the fringes of the nearby forest. His garden provided carrots, potatoes and a few other hardy root crops that could survive the unpredictable late spring and early fall frosts.

As the work progressed and one day wound itself into another, John's food supplies came up short just a few items, the most serious of which was coffee. He determined to make a quick trip to the Lewis home and then, on his way back to stop at High River for supplies. On his way out he stopped at the Quirk ranch to see what they might be in need of. One neighbor helping and caring for another was the way of the frontier.

The Ware Ranch had been established on Sheep Creek for almost one full year. As 1890 turned into 1891 the news of the territory was all of changes, and the events of the recent past. But as he rarely left the ranch during the cold months, John had heard very little about the happenings around him.

After a quick ride to the Lewis farm, he

stopped in High River where he gathered up the few items he needed. On the way home he visited his friends at the Quorn and Bar U ranches. There, at each stop, he picked up some news. And indeed, much had changed and was still changing.

Perhaps the biggest and most important news was that the Blackfoot Chief of Chiefs, the great warrior and peacemaker, and acknowledged Indian leader, Crowfoot, had died. This was the man who welcomed the Mounted Police to his territory when the whiskey traders were the source of the bottled horror that had wreaked such devastation on the Bands. It was Crowfoot that held the bands together and who had kept, for the most part, peace between the People and the encroaching ranchers. What would happen with his death was a worry.

John, living so close to the mountains and the Blackfoot Band's foothills sanctuary, took the warnings he received seriously.

For ranchers, their concerns were the serious drop in the price in the beef market. When the British government found an excuse to place an embargo on Canadian beef, mostly to satisfy their own voting, farm constituents, the cattlemen took a serious blow to their incomes.

To add to their woes, the far away national

government, in their collective ignorance of conditions on the ground, were continuing to encourage homesteading on land that would never grow a crop under the natural conditions of wind and low rainfall. There had been some small experimentation with irrigation but effective use of it was still far in the future.

Although a major range war was averted, there were smaller incidents of fence cutting, cattle being pushed through planted crops and a general unwelcome for the farmers. The settlers responded with grass fires and burned haystacks. In the end, most farmers were defeated, not by the ranchers, but by the weather and soil conditions. One after another they pulled out, leaving plowed-under grass, sagging remnants of barb wire fencing and broken fields as their lasting legacy.

On a positive note, for the ranchers who had spent large sums of money importing purebred bulls and quality beef cows, was the imposition of customs regulations and the quarantine on incoming cattle. It was hoped these measures would slow down the spread of scrub bulls wandering the country and put a stop to the importing of tick infested longhorns and longhorn crosses. With the days of the longhorn having essentially ended years before, the laws and regulations were late in coming, as was typical of government, but were welcomed by the ranchers anyway.

In just a little over one decade the number of cattle on the Alberta grasslands, that had so recently been home to untold numbers of migrating buffalo, had risen from nothing to an estimated one hundred thousand head. In addition to that number were the tens of thousands of sheep. The range was well and truly settled.

The north of the province was being settled as well. Spur rail lines were run from Calgary, north to Edmonton and south to Fort Macleod. Thousands of land-seeking immigrants were taking up homesteads on the more heavily treed lands to the north where the black loam soil was deeper, and crops could easily be grown.

John listened to this news and thought to himself that his little spread on the Sheep, holding just two hundred cows and their calves, wouldn't have much impact on where the country was headed. But those few animals would most certainly have an impact on where he was headed, and the young lady he hoped and prayed would become a part of the entire adventure.

At the Quorn, when he was told that

Stanley Pinhorn, manager of the Oxley ranch had taken his own life, in shock, John whipped off his hat and held it before him, with his work-hardened hands twisting the pressed felt like a dampened rag.

"Why for he do that?"

John Barter answered, somewhat solemnly, "There's no telling, John. Every man fights his own personal and internal battles. Stan's battles must have looked too big for him to face. We'll never know for sure. But we will miss Stan. He was a good cattleman and a good man."

John had, perhaps, his biggest surprise, mostly because of his person knowledge of the company, when he got to town and was told that the I. G. Baker Company, the venerable old supplier to ranchers, miners, farmers and travelers, had sold out to the Hudson Bay Company.

Riding on to the Ware Ranch, John's head was spinning with news.

CHAPTER 23

During the warming weeks of spring John alternated between long, lonesome hours in the saddle watching over the bulls and yearlings that had been turned out to graze, and the care of the still fenced-in cows and young calves that needed protection from coyotes, wolves, bears and the odd cougar. The cows and calves wouldn't be turned out onto grass until they had a better chance of protecting themselves, although there would always be risks. When the cattle were looked after he got his garden planted.

Intent again on a quick trip to visit the Lewis home, John bathed and put on the best clothing he owned, none of which would pass inspection at a fancy-dress ball, and rode to the Quirk homestead.

"Hello, John." John Ware hollered, "You in dat barn or you off ta town or you be hav'n de nap?"

The response, "Good morning, John,"

came from the small barn, followed by the smiling face of John Quirk.

The two men often had fun with their names. "Too many Johns on this grass, my friend. And then when we add in John Barter and the illusive John Turner, who I have not yet seen nor met, I'm thinking someone needs to admit to a second or middle name that could be used, just to relieve the confusion, you understand."

The two of them would laugh at the idea and then forget it until the thought was repeated, weeks or months later.

"Where you headed to, John, all spiffed up like that? Just out for a ride in the sun or are you going up to see your lady again?"

Leaving his small ranch in the care of the Quirks, John made the long ride to the Lewis home. There was no disguising the purpose of his visits, although John was wise enough to include Dan Lewis and Mildred's mother in his conversation.

John would not have considered himself a judge of the Lewis attempt at small scale farming. But looking at the situation as it appeared on the surface, at least, the family was barely meeting their costs of living. Using the excuse of not wishing to be a burden, he had carefully wrapped a hind leg of elk in a piece of canvas and tied it behind the saddle. Mrs. Lewis tried to downplay the importance of the gift but the look on her face told the tale.

John had one great fear in his pursuit of Mildred, one he could not possibly do anything about. His age was against him. Even by pioneer standards, where men were quite often older than their wives, the gap between him and Mildred would be seen as considerable. Was she simply playing a game? Was he no more than a diversion from the isolation of a small farm on a sparsely settled but growing frontier? Did she welcome his attention simply because he was black, as she was, and she had made no other real friends who could help fill the hours?

He decided that ignoring the situation was his best approach, hoping all the while that neither Mildred nor her parents would make an issue of the age difference, and that Mildred's welcome was truly genuine.

Thinking and believing the best, he would continue the visits until an outcome was accomplished, either positive or negative.

John concerned himself about how many times he could ask the Quirks to care for his ranch while he rode off courting Mildred, who he was firmly convinced was the love of his life. John Quirk scoffed at the idea of restricting the rides to Calgary and encouraged John in his pursuits. Much relieved, John made several more trips that summer and fall, as his work allowed. With each visit he was careful to bring a gift. As the family appeared to find the addition of wild meat to be a treat on their table, as often as not, there was a piece of elk or venison tied behind the saddle. But just one family sized stew made from a black bear that had been pestering the young calves was enough to convince John that, although he enjoyed the somewhat pungent change from time to time, bear would never be a favorite at the Lewis residence. He would stick to the tried-and-true elk.

As freeze-up was upon the small farm, John loaded a whole side of elk onto a second horse. Together he and Dan Lewis cut and wrapped it, storing the prepared meat in a covered box buried in the snow, ready for winter's use.

An invitation for a Christmas visit seemed to John to present the perfect opportunity for a serious discussion between himself and Mildred. After planning his approach to Mildred and clearing, once again, with the neighbors for the care of the Ware Ranch, John saddled up on a cold December morning. The ride to the Lewis farm would take a good part of the limited winter sunlight. On a quick side-trip into town, John, ever conscious of the dwindling coins in his possession, found a small gift he hoped Mildred would enjoy having.

John was welcomed by the entire family. He put his horse up in the small barn and, after caring for the hard ridden animal, made his way to the warmth of the house and the wood fired cast iron kitchen range. The visit went well but John's plan was stymied a bit with the realization that the weather was too cold for an evening's walk in the snow. The small house allowed little room for privacy. The courting couple, both seeming to sense the importance of the occasion, were faced with a dilemma.

The Lewis family, trying not to be too obvious with their actions, but also recognizing the situation, begged off more visiting, and with expressions of great weariness, took to their own beds. John and Mildred were left alone in the warm kitchen. Over the next hour John expressed his caring for Mildred and, with the quietest and most tender voice he could dig out of his usual boisterous vocal cords, explained his situation with the ranch and the cattle. With two hundred breeding cows, most just recently weaned from their calves, and the previous year's yearling calves soon ready for market, plus an entire new calf crop in just a few months, John would not be considered rich, in comparison to the Bar U or the Quorn but he certainly wasn't poor.

Interspersed with the gentle talk of affection and some further explanation of John's slave past, was the talk of home and security. The talk ranged from larger matters like the growing herd of cattle, and then delved into newer and smaller things like raising chickens and milking a cow. They both laughed when it was discovered that neither one had ever milked a cow.

That they were verbally dancing around the subject they both wished to discuss placed a few moments of awkwardness into the evening. John, dragging up all the internal strength and determination he had ever used in riding a bucking horse, or in throwing a horned steer, hesitated, reached for Mildred's hand, and then stumbled through a proposal of sorts. Not really being sure where the words came from, he somehow got the message out and the critical question asked.

He finished with something like, "Oh, Miss Mildred, I not be so good wit de words. Somehow never learned to talk quite right. I be good wit de horse and de cow.

And I be pretty good wit sav'n of de money. We not be hungry if we be together. Maybe-so you be will'n . . ."

"Yes, John," Mildred, understanding the situation, smilingly interjected into John's stumbling question, "Yes, John. Maybe-so, I be willing."

The result of that time alone, followed by serious discussions between Mildred and her parents resulted in the marriage of John Ware and Miss Mildred Lewis at the Baptist church in Calgary on Feb. 29, 1892.

Following the wedding the couple made the long, cold trip back to Sheep Creek, with Mildred's few possessions and a number of needed household items purchased in Calgary, loaded into the back of John's wagon. In the small log cabin on Sheep Creek, with the Quirks as the only close-by neighbors, John and Mildred Ware set up their first home together. With much knowledge of ranching and the animals that made for success, and in spite of their dearth of knowledge about anything else resembling marriage, or of other critical domestic matters, two happier people couldn't have been found on the Alberta grasslands.

Mildred was delighted with the new sawn board built cabin, enjoying its simplicity, the wonderful countryside, the closeness of the snow topped mountains, the deer that wandered down to the hay yard hoping to get a morsel of nourishment, and married life itself. With just the two of them, and not a lot of space to clean and make a welcome in, she had a lot of spare time on her hands. She filled some of this time outside, watching as John worked with the cattle. When she wanted to go among the newly born calves John warned her off.

"Dat mamma cow what looks so sleepy and contented now, can wake up and be a mean critter, pretty quick, when someone get too close to her baby. Best you stays away for now. Maybe, come by n by, you learn more about de cows you kin help wit de work."

"Will you get me a horse and teach me to ride?"

The question came at John totally unexpected. One moment they're talking about the dangers of mixing in with the cows and calves. The next she's talking about horses and riding. John had a lot to learn about how women's minds worked. When he was too long in answering, while he sorted it all out in his mind, Mildred, now labeled Millie, took the silence wrong.

"Why, Mr. Ware. Are you afraid I might not be capable of riding a horse? Is that what you're saying?"

"I ain't said noth'n yet. Don't know where you got that idea. You smart and you strong. No reason you can't learn to ride. Sure, I teach you. Come de first day wit good weather we goin' take de wagon down to de Quorn Ranch. Der be lots a good horses der. Maybe-so dey sell us one and he be your own horse. Maybe-so dey sell us de saddle too. Dat be alright?" Millie's serious look turned into a radiant smile that caused John to wonder again how this lovely lady had managed to find her way into his life. As he had done so often, he whispered a silent prayer of thanks.

CHAPTER 24

Millie screamed as she slipped from the saddle, landing face first into a deep, soft snowdrift. Her new horse, a black gelding with four white stockings and a white slash across his forehead, sensed the instability when his feet touched on the snowy grade. Not liking the infirm footing, he had lunged into the snowdrift, with his back feet sliding on the frosty surface, and his front feet leaving the ground, before dropping suddenly into the snow. The slight downward slope of the natural grade meant that the gelding's head was lowered, and the saddle tipped downward. Not yet mastering the idea of gripping the swell of the pommel with her thighs, Millie slid forward. Before she could correct the slide, she was already sprawled across the horse's neck and head, and her feet had left the security of the stirrups. By that time, nothing was going to prevent her inevitable descent into the snow drift.

John swung off his own horse and in three or four running steps was kneeling at her side. Millie was sitting back on her folded legs by the time John reached out to help her. She was making ineffectual swipes at her snow-covered face, with her gloved hands, and blowing snow from her mouth and nostrils. Her knit woolen toque was all askew, covering both her eyes, and allowing snow to drop from the brightly colored wool and slide down her back, under her warm coat. She pushed the toque back, more or less into position, and started to laugh.

John, beside himself with concern for his lovely young bride, knelt beside her, ignoring her laughter, and said, "Do you be alright? Are you hurt?"

Saying nothing, Millie scrambled to her feet. John helped just a little bit, once he figured out what she was trying to do. The gelding, who she had named 'Beauty', stood motionless, having taken a couple of steps away after the fall. Again, blowing snow from her nostrils, and ignoring John for a moment, Millie reached out to the horse. Gently taking a bridle strap in one hand, she stroked the gelding's neck and rubbed him behind his ears, a motion he seemed to enjoy.

"Well, my Beauty, you surprised me that

time. I didn't mean to frighten you. Sorry, if I did. You're a good horse and I love you. I promise not to slide over your head again if you'll promise not to jump into any more snowdrifts."

It was all gibberish to the horse, of course, but the sound of her voice seemed to calm him.

Directing the animal with a slight tug on the bridle strap, Millie and the animal were soon on level ground again. She quickly checked the saddle, as John had shown her, placed her foot into the stirrup and swung aboard. With a bright, teasing smile she turned to her husband, who was still standing helplessly, as if he had no idea what to do or say.

"Well, are we riding or are we just going to stay here until darkness is upon us?"

John studied her smile for just a moment and then turned to his own mount.

Millie had been doing very well with her riding lessons. The tumble was just one more step along the way of learning, showing clearly that she hadn't been ready when the horse made an unexpected move. She knew John would explain her error and she would listen carefully. But right now, she was enjoying the moment and the look on his face, something between surprise and

219

pleasure. Surprise at her quick recovery and pleasure at her good nature.

"Maybe-so you be teach'n me come by n by."

"Maybe-so, my dear husband, but somehow I doubt that."

They had been riding for over two hours. The afternoon would soon be gone, and John had ranch matters to deal with before darkness covered the land. Millie turned her horse towards the cabin and said, "I'm thinking it's time for coffee and a sit by the fire while the coffee comes to a boil. And I have to get into some clothes that aren't dampened with cold and snow."

As they pulled up to the horse shed John had put together at the side of the smaller corral, Millie dismounted and started to pull the rigging from Beauty. John glanced over the saddle on his own horse and said, "You go to de house 'n' get yourself warmed up. I be tak'n care o' de horses."

Without looking at him she answered, "I've always heard that a horseman takes care of his animal first, before looking to his own comfort. I don't imagine it should be any different for a woman. Anyway, Beauty expects me to be the one who cares for him, so I do believe I have it to do. We'll be warm by the fire by n by, as you so often say."

John grinned at this woman who so recently had become his wife and said, "What I'm goin do wit' you, girl?"

"Well, Mr. Ware, I can tell you what you are not going to do. You're not going to send me back to my parents. That is simply not going to happen. There is no money back guarantee in the marriage contract. No, Mr. Ware, you are stuck with me, riding mistakes and all."

She had her back to John the whole time she had been talking so he could only assume that she was smiling as she spoke.

With the leather gear put safely away, out of the weather, the two riders took pieces of burlap sacking and gave the animals a good rubdown, John topped up the trough with hay. He carried a bucket of well water to each horse, and the newlyweds walked hand in hand to the cabin.

CHAPTER 25

As the feeling of spring was in the air, Millie watched from outside the corral as John assisted in the delivery of several calves. Thankfully, most cows needed no help. With just two hundred cows, the calving wouldn't last long but, as always, John wondered at the gaps between births, as if the bulls had taken a few days off, back all those months ago.

Insisting that she would be fine, and that it was time for her to become more involved, Millie put on an old pair of John's pants and a shirt, pushed her feet down into a pair of rubber boots they had purchased in High River, and came to the corral. The men's clothing was ridiculously oversized for her but working in the pants and shirt was better than trying to work with the cows while wearing a wide hemmed, flopping ladies' dress.

As he had earlier, John objected to her

presence among the busy, bawling cows and calves. Millie waved off his concerns with a bit of a laugh. Her eagerness to learn and be involved overcame any fear she may have held previously.

Millie was almost totally untutored on the birthing of ranch animals. The first few births she witnessed from outside the corral, fascinated her. She wanted to be personally involved and John found no way to deny her that activity, in spite of his concerns. Copying John, she climbed into the corral with a piece of torn sacking in each hand and a determination that John was to see over many years, and many situations. Even John, with his large, powerful hands was occasionally having difficulty holding on to the slippery legs of the calves as he assisted the cows. Millie would need the extra grip the sacking would provide.

As the ranching couple stood by while a calf was born without assistance, Millie said, "Alright, I've watched and now I'm going to do the job for the next mama that needs help."

Silently John was hoping that the remaining births would come easily, and they could simply stand by. But that was not to be. Later in the afternoon a cow was clearly having difficulty. When John stepped up to assist, Millie shouldered him aside and said, "No, Mr. Ware. This one is mine and you're going to teach me each step of the way."

Millie's first experience at birthing a calf was a relatively easy one, not requiring more human strength than she could provide. Still, she ended up sitting in the muck of the corral with her feet pressed firmly against the cow's rear and with her fingers gripping the calf's front legs so tightly that her hands began to shake with the exertion. John had to assist just once, as he gently guided the calf's nose into position. He commented, "If de calves' nose not be com'n correct, de head maybe-so get turned to de back and dat not be so good."

Millie's didn't really answer verbally but she nodded in acceptance of that information.

At the end of just a few minutes pulling, waiting at intervals, until the cow's contractions would again become a natural pushing action, the calf's hind quarters flopped out, landing on Millie's legs, with the placenta still half wrapped around the little body. As a sign that the birth was about to happen, the cow's water sack had broken. Within a few seconds of the calf's delivery, what water had not yet leaked out came in a surge, flooding Millie's feet and the lower portion of her legs. She was so enthralled with the new life that lay in front of her that she hardly noticed the other things that had taken place. She sat there with the melting snow and corral muck soaking into her clothing, staring at the small red body with the white face until John laughed and said, "You be de true rancher now."

"What do I do next, John?"

"You reach into de mouth and pull de tongue flat and make sure der be noth'n ta stop de little fella from breath'n. Den you get up and you leave de rest to de cow. She be lick'n him all over, cleaning off de birth'n wet and warm'n him with her rough tongue. She be want'n ta claim dis little fella for her own. You cain't no way help wit dat. Pretty soon, by n by, he get up and be look'n for his breakfast. And de Ware Ranch be hav'n de new bull calf to care for."

With the cow licking and tasting her newborn, she was identifying him as her own baby. Until he was weaned, many months from that moment, she would never forget. The calf was becoming aware of who his mother was, at the same time. After a few minutes, the cow nudged the calf, pushing him into the position where he could stand. With several false starts, all lovingly supervised by the cow, plus two curious cows that had not yet calved, the calf finally wobbled and staggered a bit and then took his first steps. The cow nudged him some more and, as if new lifegiving information was entering his mind, he bumped his head into his mother's udder and found a teat.

John, carefully watching, said, "Dat first drink be call de colostrum. De calf, he need dat to git his little body work'n proper. After dat he be hav'n jest de milk."

Millie's hand was muck covered and dirtier than it had ever been but if she even noticed, it didn't seem to matter. She slipped her hand into John's equally mucky hand and the two of them stood watching as the miracle of new life, mixed in with the hopes of future profits for their small ranch, completed itself before their eyes.

John finally turned from the cow and her calf and concentrated on his wife.

"Dat be a good job you be do'n. But now I tink you might want to go to de cabin and git yourself inta clean clothes. I'll be along by n by."

Finally, within a few days, the last calf came into the world, two more with Millie's assistance.

With the day's work put behind him, John walked to the cabin, kicked off his outdoor boots and hung up his warm coat and hat before announcing, "Every cow now hav'n de baby runn'n beside her. We not lose any dis year. Dat be good news."

Millie turned from the big, fire heated pot of elk stew she was preparing and said, "That indeed is good news. We have much to be thankful for. Now you get yourself washed up. I'm just waiting for a pan of biscuits to come out of the oven and we're ready to eat."

With the calving complete, John and Mildred made a quick, surprise visit to the Lewis home. There were many shouts of welcome and smiles all around as they rode their horses down the short grade and into the farmyard. The younger Lewis siblings made much of the fact that their older sister came all the way from the ranch astride the black horse.

"Here you come riding a horse on your first visit back to home. That's a pretty horse. Will you let me have a ride?"

Many other comments and questions were flung their way before they even dismounted. Ignoring the questions, Mildred wrapped her arms around her mother and then her father.

"It's good to see you all. How have you been? Well, I hope."

"We're all fine and it's good to see the two of you too. But that's a long ride. You must be tired. Come in and sit down. Rest a bit."

"I appreciate your sentiment, Mother, but right now, sitting down might not be my most pressing priority. I'll stand for a bit if you don't mind. Or even walk around and take a look at your garden."

Dan Lewis said, "Sit, stand, walk around, lay down for a while. Whatever. It's good to see you."

John was untying the canvas sack from behind the saddle. In addition to the sack, which contained spare clothing and a small bag of overnight necessities Mildred had put together, there was a canvas covered roll holding a couple of blankets for emergency use, plus their warm coats and rain wear.

Because Mildred was a lighter burden to her black gelding, John had tied the gift of a side of venison behind her saddle. Mildred's brother was untying the gift of meat saying, "Mother, look, John must had shot another deer. You were just saying a few days ago that you had a taste for venison. Well, here it is."

When they were all gathered around the big kitchen table, with Mildred finally taking a seat, the questions started again. When the questions about cold weather, the warmth of the cabin and finally, calving season were asked, more or less all at once by different members of the family, John smiled and answered, "I be let'n Millie tell all of dat. She be doin' all de work while I jest be rest'n and wait'n for de dinner time."

Humor had not been one of John's more obvious traits before that time. It took a few seconds for the family to appreciate his comments. But, indeed, John remained quiet while Millie answered all their questions. With the stories of falling off the horse into the snow drift and her first venture into pulling a calf, the family roared with laughter.

She completed her update by assuring the family that John had worked tirelessly and that the ranch and cattle were in good condition and ready for the summer.

To the question of how long they could stay, Millie explained the situation with John Quirk and how that good man had filled in every time he was needed. John had returned the favor on two occasions when the Quirks needed to take the wagon in to High River for supplies.

They stopped the visiting long enough for Dan to cut some venison steaks while

Mildred peeled potatoes and her mother shook up the fire in the big cast iron stove and prepared the fry pans in preparation for the steaks. She then dug into the small vegetable bin and lifted out an onion, passing it to Mildred.

"That's the last onion from all those we pulled from the garden last fall. If you'll chop it up, I believe it will go nicely with the steaks, if I give it just a few minutes in the hot pans after the steaks are done."

Mildred's sister was mixing biscuit dough. By the time the steaks were ready for the table she would be pulling the pan of biscuits from the oven.

When the meal was eaten and the dishes cleared away, the coffee pot was carried around again. With many thanks for the venison, the family pushed their chairs away from the table and the questions started again.

Mildred answered a few questions and then said, "Oh, but I must tell you about the neighbors.

"I don't really understand how news gets around out on the grasslands, as John calls it. The country is so large and the ranches so far apart. I've heard people referring to the moccasin telegraph. They tell me that's a term adopted from the Native Blackfoot people. They apparently send runners from village to village with news of the tribes. And because most of them wear moccasins, the ranchers started calling it the moccasin telegraph.

"However, it was done, somehow word was sent out all across the ranching country and a welcome party for us was arranged. They called it a housewarming. My goodness, what a surprise. We had no idea anything like that would happen. But just so we would be ready and not out riding somewhere, our friend and closest neighbor, Mr. Quirk rode over the day before. He suggested we stay close to home as there were a few folks planning a visit.

"I couldn't believe so many people would take an entire day away from their ranches and ride so far to visit and welcome us. It was a beautiful spring day, so the men mostly stayed outside, leaning on the corral fencing, looking at the cattle and telling stories. There are still a lot of single ranchers, so there were fewer ladies but my, the food and fixings they brought.

"Our little cabin couldn't have held any more people. If the weather had turned rainy and all those men had come inside, we would have been packed out.

"The ladies insisted that they would do all

the work and that I simply meet each person and visit, getting to know the neighbors.

"My goodness, couples arrived in wagons with prepared food wrapped up in the back. Even single men brought something, tied behind their saddle. Because they all wanted to get home that evening, they came at lunch time. What a spread those ladies put out. My, my! Then, shortly after lunch, they headed home. Some wouldn't make it home that evening. They would stay with other ranchers along the way.

"We had a glorious time. What a fine bunch of folks. Now, I have to be honest with myself. I don't really think they came for me, although I'm sure that was a part of it. More curiosity than anything perhaps. It's likely that most of them have never spoken to a black woman before and, possibly, John is the only black man they have ever known.

"The men showed no sign of hesitation about coming into a black woman's house, but I did notice a couple of the ladies were just a bit uncertain. It didn't take them long to get past that and pitch in to help and to visit.

"But what was clear is that the ranchers hold John very high in their minds. I heard stories with much laughter as the men told of John's exploits, most of which I had never heard before. John was pretty uncomfortable about it all, but he took it in good grace.

"It was a great day. One I will never forget. The distances, and the fact that John has no hired man to do the work if we're away, will hold us back from returning many of the visits but we'll do what we can."

In the stillness of the evening, as Mildred was quietly discussing the family matters with her mother while they washed and dried the dishes, Mildred said, "Mother. Tell me the truth. Are you making a living on this little piece of land?"

Her mother's hesitancy, as she concentrated on the wash water before her, was really all the answer Mildred needed. But she waited quietly while her mother searched for words. When she finally spoke it was to say, "The winter was very hard. In the cold weather the chickens stopped laying, so we had nothing to sell. Your father went to the city looking for carpentry work, but none of the contractors offered anything. They all said the same thing, 'wait for spring'. All he could find was day labor, and none of that was steady work. We're a long way from Calgary if he had to travel in each day, and the pay wouldn't even cover a small room and some food in the city, so he gave up on that. Perhaps there will be work in the spring.

"He's done some work for a neighbor and that helped. We get by."

Mildred said no more, knowing that saving her mother's pride had a value too. But she was determined to return soon with more meat, and possibly a bit of money as a gift, if John followed through on his plan to sell a couple of calves to purchase chickens and a milk cow.

She didn't know until they were almost home, that John had slipped her father a few dollars when they were outside, visiting alone.

Chapter 26

Mildred wasn't really happy about it, but John's reputation as a steer wrestler, horse rider and overall strong man started to gain a larger audience. As mid-summer approached, the organizers of the Calgary summer fair sent a rider to talk with John. He was wanted at the fair to show his skills and entertain the crowds. There would be a bit of money in it for him.

Mildred objected, saying that their little ranch was doing well, but that it still needed John's constant attention. She was correct, of course, but John argued that the cattle were fine, fending for themselves on the range, and that most of the predators appeared to be under control, by numbers, if not by deeds.

"We's be goin' to see your Daddy and Mama first, den we go to de city. Maybe-so some of your family, dey come wit us. We be back home in jest a few days."

And so they went. John was the crowning performer in a weekend of fun, food, and what would become, in a few years, one of the premier rodeos in the world. Millie was terrified, watching her husband take on one of the largest horned steers anyone had ever seen. She had been assured by John before the event, that there would be riders close by in case something went wrong.

When the time for the steer wrestling came, John eased up to the side of the animal and nodded to the riders to loosen their hold ropes. The steer, having no love for horses, riders or confinement, and certainly not for this creature that was hanging onto his horns, decided to run for the open range.

John's grip was firm and steady, and his boot heels were dug deeply into the sand of the competition ring. Still, with the steer lunging and twirling in a circle, John was cast about like a flag in the wind. But every time he landed he forced his heels back into the sand. Finally, slowly, with full concentration on the task, with his arm muscles bulging and knotting with effort, and with his considerable weight leaning down and toward the left, John managed to start turning the steer's massive head. With the turn extended, the horns now pointing upward and downward, instead of side to side, John released his right hand from the horn and grabbed the monster's jaw. Now, with the steer standing in one place, unable to run in the position John had forced him into, John swung his left hand to grasp the upper horn. With the twisting on the jaw plus the pulling on the horn the steer was overbalanced. The fight was really over but the steer didn't know that yet. With a few more frantic kicks and a bellow heard throughout the stadium, and with John forcing compliance with a final muscular heave, the animal fell to his side. John nimbly stepped out of the way before falling across the steer's neck to hold him down. The applause was deafening. After John made a mental count of five seconds he leaped back to his feet, strolled away and smiled up at Millie. The steer was left to the care of the riders.

Looking up into the stands and listening to the cheering, John couldn't help contrasting that day with his first visit to Calgary, where he was treated so rudely and roughly. It was true that a few years had gone by, and the city had grown with a lot of new immigrants arriving, but in John's mind, it wasn't that many years and the memories were still hurtfully fresh.

After the steer wrestling, the horse bucking competition almost seemed tame, but John put all his efforts into that as well and won the event.

A couple of days later, riding home, Millie said, "John, I don't want you to be doing that anymore. I can't imagine losing you. And you would have to admit that there is considerable risk in what you did. I like you as a rancher. I'm not sure I would like you as an entertainer.

"Now, I know you did very well, and the other competitors tried their hardest, so you won fair and square. And, of course, you have a bit of money you didn't have last week. But I'm not so sure the cheering wasn't nearly as much from the novelty of watching a black man, kind of like a Vaudeville show, as it was about you showing what you could do."

Millie had to take a couple of minutes explaining what a Vaudeville show was. John had never heard the term.

After explaining about the public entertainment offered by the shows, she said, "I saw one of the travelling shows back east. They had travelled up from New York. The thing is, John, in that show the blacks were treated almost like pets, or playthings. It was like they were people put on this earth to entertain the whites and be laughed at.

"The singers and dancers were all white folks with blackening on their faces, putting the idea forward that they were black themselves. But many of our people can sing or dance every bit as well, and probably better than most of the ones hiding behind black shoe polish.

"You are not someone's pet, John, like you were a horse or a dog. You're a man. Maybe the best man I've ever known, black or white. And you're my husband. And you're going to be the father of our children, perhaps sooner than you expect."

Millie was trying to tell John something with the last statement but, with his mind on the show, the prize money in his pocket and the long ride ahead of him, plus planning the work he would be doing, somehow the message bounced off his ears. Millie decided to let it go until she was sure of her condition. It might be just as well. If she got John all excited about being a father and it turned into a false alarm he would feel terribly let down. Yes, she would wait.

John was silent for a long time but finally he looked right at Millie with a wide grin and said, "Dat man what was runn'n de fair, he gave me forty dollars."

Millie returned his smile. "I know he did, John, and I also know you gave half of it to my father. That was very kind of you. So, I forgive you for scaring me half to death when you were wrestling that huge steer. But that doesn't mean I ever want you to be doing that again."

CHAPTER 27

Although ranchers and farmers had for generations, been known to be independent, stalwart and private men, most of them still longed for a wife or sons who could help around the place and add purpose to his lonely life.

There are things that need doing that simply require a third hand or another bit of muscle when the rancher is at the end of his own strength. It was at those times that neighbors were called upon. John was fortunate to have Millie to assist in his times of need, and, of course, the Quirks and John had worked closely together from the start.

As independent as the ranchers were, there were still those times that a man would arrive at the Ware Ranch expressing a need. And John never failed to ride off, prepared to do what he could for friends and neighbors.

The sharing of work on the Ware Ranch

and the neighboring one-man spreads had John riding away from home more often than either he or Millie liked. But for small ranchers to survive and prosper it was, from time to time, necessary for a man to seek the assistance of another able-bodied male. John had benefited from the help of others, and he was happy to offer his help in return.

Following one excursion to help a neighbor with some branding, John and his neighbor, John Quirk rode into sight of the home place with a wave and a shouted, "Hey you, ranch. Is anybody to home?"

Millie poked her head out of the small barn and waved a greeting, before saying, with a smile, "My husband isn't home. You'll have to come back later if you wish to see him."

"What yo talk'n bout woman? He be home now. And you be look'n mighty good to him." John was getting used to Millie's sense of humor and to returning her smiles with one of his own.

The newness of their love hadn't yet worn off. Millie hoped it never would. There had yet to be a time that she watched John ride down that slope into their yard that she, again, thanked God for putting the two of them together.

With a wave at Millie, John Quirk rode onward, knowing that his wife would be watching for his arrival too. Millie returned to the barn while John corralled and cared for his horse. He laid his saddle onto the frame built for it and walked over to where Millie was brushing Beauty. The horse appeared to enjoy every stroke of the brush. John approached her from behind and slipped his arms around her, giving her a hug.

"You look'n mighty good to me there, Millie girl. I sure be glad to be to home."

Millie leaned back into his embrace and said nothing. John wondered if there was something wrong. She was usually much more talkative than that.

He was silent for a moment and then said, "You be car'n for dis horse might fine. Always you be brush'n and clean'n and talk'n to him. But you not be rid'n much anymore."

John didn't like silences between himself and Millie. Thankfully, the silences were seldom, usually meaning that either there was something wrong or that Millie had a thought on her mind and was unsure about how to express herself. And usually, by this time on his return rides she had offered coffee and perhaps a late lunch, in case he hadn't eaten yet. But there had been no mention of coffee or lunch. That was a sure sign that her mind was somewhere else.

"You be think'n bout someth'n girl."

Struggling to drag up her last bit of courage, Millie finally said, "I've been thinking about how you would like to be a father."

Taken totally by surprise, John answered quickly, indicating that he hadn't really heard the message or hadn't thought it through.

"I be lik'n dat jest fine."

There was silence again, just a few seconds.

"Wait a minute, girl. Be you tell'n me . . . ?"

"Yes. I tried to tell you before but then I wasn't real sure. But now I am. You are going to be a daddy."

John smiled from ear to ear and turned Millie around to face him.

"And dat means you goin' be a Mama. Why dat be jest fine. Jest fine and good. Praise de Lawd. I be prais'n de Lawd for you, girl."

CHAPTER 28

Bill Moodie, still on the payroll of the Bar U, was a welcome, but unexpected visitor on the Ware Ranch. He had been there just the once before at the welcoming party. To see him again so soon told John immediately that he was coming with news. No one rode such distances on the grasslands without a purpose.

On seeing his old friend riding down the gentle slope into the ranch yard, he stepped out of the corral and stood waiting. The two men would normally be shouting their greetings but when Bill approached silently, John held his peace.

Finally, close enough to speak in a normal voice, Bill held up his hand in greeting and said, "Morn'n, John. Hope all is well with you and the Missus."

"Fine. Fine out here on dis little place Bill. Step down and tell me what bring'n you all dis way on dis sunny day."

Bill stepped to the ground and the two men shook hands. Bill could see no purpose in holding back on the news, so he quietly said, "Got some bad news, John. Just heard last evening. Ol' Tom Lynch is dead. His wife found him dead in his bed. Apparently, he had been feeling poorly for some days but kept on with his work. Must have been more serious than he thought."

The two men stood in silence while their memories rolled back across the years. Finally, Bill said, "Lost one of the best with Tom gone. Good at everything he ever put his hand to. Trail driver, rancher, cattleman, friend, Boss. Dreamer. He was a man who dreamed big dreams. Saw the size of these grasslands and the possibilities, maybe before anyone else did. He called it for cattle and horse country right from the start. Tried to tell everyone who would listen that plowing this wonderful grass under was a mistake. An unfixable mistake, he warned, that time would bring us to regret. Trouble was, not many would listen. But in the years since, we've seen the wisdom he tried to share."

John listened silently, with his eyes cast to the ground. In his mind was the day Tom had called him out of the drive, away from the plodding cattle, to show him the rock cairn at the border.

"He be shown' me de rock pile what mark de border of dis country. Explain to me what dat meant. He ask me about where I be from. Who my Papa and my Mama be. Where dey are now. He be a good man. Maybe-so he be sleep'n too many cold nights on de ground. Maybe-so he be hurt too many times on de job. Maybe-so, his body jest be tired. Dis not be a easy life. Hard on de man and de horses, both. Maybe-so it jest be de time fo' him ta take de rest. Only de Lawd know what dat time be fo' each man."

The good lunch put on the table by Millie, and the bottomless coffee pot shared by the three of them worked together to cast some of the gloom off the sad news. Before long the two men were laughing as they told Tom Lynch stories. That the laughter was a covering over the real hurts, was a way of coping for hard working and lonely men spread so thinly across the grasslands.

After another short time of visiting, Bill saddled up and swung aboard his gelding. The two men shook hands and Bill thanked Millie again with a wave. John and Millie watched their friend ride back towards the Bar U, knowing that it might be months before they met again. And who was to say they would ever meet again? Tom Lynch. Strong, wise, hardworking Tom was gone. Gone the way of all flesh. Any one of them could be the next to be called home.

After the summer's demonstration of steer wrestling, the good folks of Calgary decided that an annual fair would be in order. The planning began and proceeded over the long winter of 1892 - 93.

Dan Lewis had found employment as a carpenter in Calgary. The family sold the small holding south of town and moved to the big city. There, in the back bedroom of the small house, Amanda Ware, later to be called Nettie, the first-born daughter to John and Mildred Ware, was born on March 9th, 1893.

John was ecstatic. As he remembered all those lonely years before Millie had come into his life, he could hardly believe that he now had a true family; husband, wife and a little one. And perhaps there would be more little ones in the future. He couldn't know about that. He was nearing fifty years of age. He didn't know his age for sure because no one could recall the exact month or year of his birth. Perhaps his parents, never having learned to read or write, had no way of marking down the date, or it was lost as additional children came into the family or possibly, they hadn't seen it as important. Living as slaves, with no freedoms at all, perhaps merely being alive was enough.

Those early years were all fading in John's memory, replaced by the better remembrances of the many friends he had made along his journey and now, the newer reality of the good grasslands he had been directed to. His little spread on Sheep Creek with its growing cattle herd, and now, a little girl to round out his life, his and Millie's lives, he corrected himself, was the ultimate reality to hold in his memory.

Keeping with the custom of the day, the young mother was kept in bed for several days, believing she would be too weak to trust herself to walk or work, and fearing that she may drop the baby in a weakened moment. John made the long ride back to the ranch by himself. With the cattle in the corral and the calving season soon upon him, he couldn't stay away. As it was, he had leaned on the services of his new neighbor, E. D. Adams. The two men had worked together for many days putting Adams' corrals and catch pens together and then tackled the small barn and finally, the house. Although the house was little more

249

than a shack, demonstrating that neither man would ever find employment as a carpenter, Adams was delighted.

"It's all great, John. Someday I'll have a good new cabin built and you and I can stand by while I burn this one to the ground, ready to make coffee over the hot coals."

Considering the costs of cut lumber, John knew he was joking. No one burned good cut lumber that could be used again, but he went along with the laughter anyway.

When Adams was asked to care for John's cow herd, throwing hay across the fence each morning and seeing that the windmill had pumped the holding tank full, he didn't hesitate.

"I'd do it anyway, my friend, but after you're all back home, if it included one of Mrs. Ware's good beef dinners, why, I'd smile for a week."

It was two weeks before John returned for his wife and child. His team and wagon had been left in Calgary, ready for the return trip. Millie was now up and feeling fine. The baby was apparently gaining weight properly, although John couldn't see much difference.

The Lewises had another guest for dinner the evening before John and Millie were to leave for Sheep Creek, another man from the east. It turned out that the gentleman, a white man, had known the Lewises back at their former home. The fellow was an educator of some kind. Knew a lot of history. That brought about a discussion on the settlement of the west and the difference between the American and the Canadian experiences.

John had little to say, knowing nearly nothing at all about the subject. He listened as the two educated men discussed the early explorers, the fur trade with the Indians, the surveyors and mappers.

"Great men of vision," said Dan Lewis.

"Perhaps greater than we can understand," was the response from Mr. Weiss.

That man leaned back in his chair, stared at the ceiling for a moment, as if trying to recollect the details, and then said, "David Thompson. Young Englishman indentured to the Hudson Bay Company in 1784. Sailed the Atlantic and arrived at Churchill to work at the fur trading post. Over time and with considerable experience with the Native folks, Thompson was made a full-time surveyor. He transferred his allegiance to the North West Company, a competitor to the old HBC company, but he stayed on good relations with them all. The man's inherent understanding of geography, the stars and the earth's landmass was, and remains unequalled. He travelled staggering distances across the west. Explored and mapped the main passes through the Rocky Mountains. Discovered and mapped the source of the great Columbia River and paddled its full length to the Pacific. First white man to ever do that. He had a friendly way with the Indians. Stopped at villages all along the Columbia leaving gifts of tobacco and making friends. The company established a string of fur trading posts along the Columbia following Thompson's successful explorations.

"Married a half breed girl. Together they had a large family. Lived in Montreal later in life. Lived in sad obscurity in his last years, much to the shame of an ungrateful nation. Or, I should probably say, to the shame of the British overlords who saw so little real value in what they loved to refer to as the 'colonies'. Died without ever receiving the recognition he so richly deserved. Sold his precious surveying instruments to purchase food. Died practically unknown and buried in an unmarked grave. No one seems to know why none of his family stepped in to assist.

"A great man treated badly at the end. But his maps are still the best available, and his calculation of the land mass and the courses of the rivers are unparalleled. He was the best that ever was. Maybe the best that ever will be. I'm hoping the country, now no longer a colony, and his fellow cartographers, remember him with more kindness than what he experienced at the end of his life."

John was lost for most of that short walk through history, but he did ask one question.

"Why it be all dis grass be here wit no cows? Montana have de cows, but not so much on dis grass. Dat be back when I first come here I's talk'n 'bout."

Dan Lewis nodded to Mr. Weiss, as if he should provide an answer. Dan knew the answer himself, but he was deferring to the more educated white man, probably a lifelong habit.

"Well, John. That's a great question. I take it you have not travelled across the country."

"No, sir. I travelled across de country many miles to de south. Down to Carolina and den to Texas. Came to here from Texas."

"Yes. Well, it's quite a different situation. Where the way west is more or less open on the American side of the international border, that is, the forty ninth parallel, the situation on the northern portion of the continent is another matter.

"Between the settled portion of Canada and this wonderful west, lie the great lakes. In particular, Lake Superior, really an inland sea, separates east from west. In addition, the land mass to the north of the lake is what is called the Precambrian Shield, or the Canadian Shield. The Shield is an unbelievable beautiful, rocky terrain stretching from the Arctic Circle right down to the border and, in a few places, pushing itself into a couple of US States. The Shield is dotted with hundreds of lakes. It is totally impenetrable by wagon. A man on horseback could get through but it would be difficult. And to bring a family and possessions would be out of the question.

"The early fur traders came by canoe, crossing the big lakes and then following rivers and portages through the chain of lakes until they reached the open western lands. They then followed the northern river route to the trading posts. It was a trip of months, requiring great human stamina and strength. Not to be undertaken by the weak or unprepared.

"The railway finally managed to dynamite a path through the rocks, but it took years and cost an enormous amount of money.

"Anyone desiring to come west years ago

would always go south into the American territories and follow the much easier Missouri River route. Even then, not many came this way. There was no real need to come west for land or opportunity. There is still a lot of land available in the East. Our total population is but a fraction of that south of the border. Canada has no big teeming cities that would match the likes of New York. So, as you can easily see and understand, there was simply no real need to come west.

"If I understand the history and situation correctly, John, and as an example of what I am talking about, the first quality cattle brought from Ontario into this land came by way of the Missouri River, which is an entirely American route with no parallel in Canada."

John had heard of that. He simply nodded in understanding.

The evening and the good talk moved along until the baby started to fuss. In the small house there was little privacy. When Millie looked directly into John's eyes, he understood it was time to turn down the lamp and bid goodnight. He stood to his feet and shook Mr. Weiss's hand.

"It be good to know you sir. We be leav'n early in de morn'n. De baby, she be need'n to feed and get de sleep. Maybe so de same for Mrs. Ware and me."

Mr. Weiss took the hint, thanked Mrs. Lewis for the dinner and left.

CHAPTER 29

The large-scale settlement on the Alberta grasslands was barely one decade old. It was in 1882 that Tom Lynch and George Emerson trailed their first, experimental herd from Montana, finding a small, but steady market around Fort Macleod. From there the cattle industry had grown with new herds arriving each year. New ranches were established on twenty-one-year land leases.

The wild longhorns running loose on Texas grass had presented an unusual opportunity for the early ranchers in that southern area. It was possible to establish a cattle ranch with very little cash. But it was not that way for those who settled other areas where no longhorns existed. Although the longhorn animals were still being driven throughout the country, becoming the original breeding stock for many ranches, the animals could no longer be had without cost.

While a few small independent operations had been able to make a modest start, the large Canadian ranches were often financed with huge amounts of capital, raised from risk-taking eastern or foreign investors.

The situation on the Alberta grasslands was similar to what had taken place on the American grasslands. Foreign investments were a frequent factor in both newly settling countries. It was common for the large ranches to have a resident manager while the true owners lived far away, in a big eastern city, in Britain or on the continent.

In the short ten years since Lynch had pushed the first Montana cattle across the 49th parallel, ranching had gone from cowboys herding their animals while they themselves slept on the ground and ate whatever they could put together over an open fire, to luxurious homes, multiple huge barns and corrals and visiting royalty from the old countries.

The working cowboys now slept in bunkhouses and sat at tables overseen by a cook.

Nowhere had a land and an industry changed so rapidly. John Ware had been there to see it all and to be a part of it all.

Sometimes, after a day of work, with the baby tucked safely into her little bed, and with the lamp turned low, and the wood stove fighting off the evening's chill, Millie would ask John about the earlier years.

"Der be no city. No big town. No good trails. No railway. Der be noth'n but de grass. So far as a fella could see was all grass. And off to de west was de mountains and de forests. And maybe-so along de creeks and de rivers more forest. But mostly der be de grass. Look'n to de east or de south, it be like as if der be noth'n in de whole world but de grass. De cows and de horses be buried to der bellies in de grass.

"Pretty soon come more cows. And den de sheep. Ol' Tom Lynch, he drive more to here but I not go wit' him. I stay on de grass and work for de rancher. First, I be work fer is de Bar U. Dat ranch not be called de Bar U when it start. Mr. Stimson, he call it de North West Cattle Company but pretty soon it be jest called de Bar U.

"Lots of de first animals, dey die in de winter storms. Snow like no one ever see before. And cold and wind. De men and de animals all be suffer'n wit de cold. Der was much for de ranchers to learn. Now, wit de hay ready for de winter, not so many animals lost to de cold.

"Der be a lot of new people come and bring money wit dem. De ranches, dey hav'n new owners. De men I ride wit in de

259

early years, many be gone. Some still be here. Some I see on de roundups but de big roundups not be needed no more. Ranchers, dey keep der animals to home. Some ranches, dey hav'n to put up de wire fences to keep der cows to home and de other animals out.

"De government, dey break der word on de leases. Open de land fer homestead'n, fer grain grow'n. Some ranchers quit and move to new grass. Maybe-so one day we hav'n to move too, find new grass."

Millie listened to all of this and responded, "I don't want to move, John. I like it here. The country is beautiful with the mountains and the forests and the deer and elk that come down to water or sneak a bit of cut hay. Our holding is smaller than the Quorn and the Bar U, but we are making a good living and we have friends around us. Where are we going to find better friends than John and Mrs. Quirk, or Mr. Adams?"

John reached for his wife's hand and said, "We be stay'n jest so long as we can, girl. But our cows be eatn' grass dat de Ware Ranch not own, jest like all de other ranches. It be called public lands. Means it be owned by de government. Maybe-so, by n by der be someone buy'n dat land. Den where our cows goin' ta find de grass?"

CHAPTER 30

John's concern about newcomers taking over the free-range lands was valid. Although Millie kept hoping that they would be left alone to live out the lives they were enjoying so much, John could see that they would be faced with the problem more quickly than even he had originally guessed. Ranchers and farmers, large and small, continued to take up homestead lands. Homestead settlers now numbered in the thousands across the grasslands and in the bush covered land to the north of the province. Every train from the east seemed to offload rail cars of newcomers. This was in addition to the steady flow of American families pointing their wagons and their herds north, towards a new start and fresh hope. The numbers of newcomers staggered the imaginations of those staunch individuals who had first ventured onto the grass. Perhaps the first vision of the land had turned into a dream that could not be sustained. But few were willing to accept that.

The dilemma of the original ranch settlers was a topic of discussion whenever neighbors got together. In a territory so large, and with most ranches remote from any settlement where accurate news could be gathered, rumor and speculation ran high.

Also running high were the emotions of the open-range ranchers, as well as the failure rate of those who turned the wonderful grass under, hoping to harvest a crop of wheat. As time was going to confirm, this windy, sunny land in the eastern shadow of the magnificent Rockies would require irrigation before marketable crops could be depended upon. The ranchers looked at the abandoned homestead plots, with their turned-over sod and the wind blowing away the loose soil, and the bent-over fence posts loosely connected with a tangle of barb wire, with a mix of anger and frustration.

The arguments of the ranchers were expressed loudly, if ineffectually, wherever the men gathered. A common complaint, and a true one, was expressed as, "Once you turn the sod down, boys, she's gone and no power on earth can bring her back. There's never been better grasslands found anywhere I ever heard of, and these fools are killing it."

By carefully conserving the graze on his own holding while herding his cattle and horse herds as far into the foothill and forest lands as he dared, John held the ranch together and kept it prosperous for several years. His own small experiment with irrigation on his hay land had proven that with that bit of diverted water he could depend on a winter's supply of feed. Some years in the past, when the rains hadn't come, the result was inadequate haystacks, and underfed animals, before the warming winds again melted the snow, to expose the luxuriant grass that lay beneath. It was a lesson John was to remember.

That the government people overseeing the settlement of the land couldn't figure the same thing out was a disappointment.

John watched and waited. He and John Quirk and their mutual friend, Adams, plotted and planned and hoped, as one year passed into another. But in 1902 he had to face reality. The homesteaders and the town builders were an unstoppable force. Their numbers alone would name them as unbeatable victors in the scramble for land.

"Millie, girl, we goin' to have to move. Find new grass. Or keep just de cows and horses dis place have grass for. Neighbors, dey be hav'n de same problem."

"What do you have in mind, John? You know I don't want to move. Is there another option? Could we purchase more land? Could we live well with fewer animals? No one in the world needs as many horses as we have, eating that precious grass. Would it be wiser to sell off a hundred or so and save the grass for the money-making cattle? And anyway, where can we go that won't eventually have the same problems we have here?"

"Millie, we have talked 'bout all of dat before. Many times, we talk."

With that, the couple went over the questions and the options again. At the end of the discussion, it was reluctantly decided that selling their Sheep Creek property and moving the ranch to more wide-open grasslands that would not be so attractive to homesteaders, was their only option.

Rather than take weeks away from Ware Ranch in an exploration of his own, John sought out men who had ridden the lands to the east, seeking their knowledge. He rode to Calgary and talked with the government people there. He asked questions wherever he found knowledgeable people. The result of all the discussions was to choose the lands north of the new town of

Brooks, Alberta, a small settlement that sprang up around the needs of the railway, as their new home. The available grassland lay along the south side of the Red Deer River.

In explaining the decision to Millie, John said, "It be drier land. Not so good for de grain grow'n. Maybe-so der be irrigation from de river, by n by. But now de grass be good for de cattle. De government man, he call it de 'short grass country'. Means dat de grass be not so tall as dis around here. But be good for de animals. And not so many people be mov'n der yet."

In every land and at every time in history there has arisen the exact man or just the right woman who fits the calling. The leaders, whether or not they saw themselves in that light. As far back in history as a person wishes to go these men stand out, with no replacements in sight. There was just one king in the cradle of civilization like Nebuchadnezzar. No back up general that could take Alexander's place when he died unexpectedly. Only one Moses who could lead millions of people in spite of his lack of self-confidence. No stand-in for John the Baptist who sent out a call for repentance and baptized thousands. And so, it went through history. There was only one Joan of Arc, One Luther, one Florence Nightingale.

At the right time in history the men who gathered a brave crew and set forth in tiny sailing vessels to explore the world, were of that type. Men of vision, taking risks and paying the price when it didn't go well and, often as not, watching others receive the glory for what they, themselves had accomplished.

In the building of the nations, it was the same. There would have never been the nation of Canada without John A. MacDonald. In the US, a man named Lincoln rose to the task when probably no other could do the job. These men and women of history weren't perfect. They made mistakes. Not everyone loved them. But no one could replace them.

And so it was with the Canadian West; a new country, jammed between the great inland seas in the east and the almost impenetrable Rocky Mountains to the west. An open, unpopulated country, although the original native inhabitants could, and did, argue the point.

Who but Colonel James F. Macleod could have led an inexperienced, largely unprepared group of young men across a thousand miles of unfamiliar territory and suc-

266

cessfully establish law and order on the great Canadian frontier, without firing a shot? And in the process, rid the country of the Fort Benton whiskey traders and convince the Indians to quit warring with their neighbors.

And who but a Jerry Potts could have come to Macleod's rescue when that band of young peacemakers found themselves hopelessly lost and running short of supplies, as they moved west on horseback, with supply wagons trailing far behind.

Was there ever a trail driver like Tom Lynch? Or an investor and cattleman who saw the possibilities of the wide-open grasslands like Fred Stimson, who was prepared to risk everything on the venture? Or a man of vision like George Emerson? Men, for it was very much a man's world in the west at that time, for whom there were no replacements. George Lane, John Barter, John Quirk, Herb Miller, Phil Weinard, Duncan Cameron, Ab Cotterell, Bill Moodie, Fred Ings, Smith and French who built The Crossing supply point when there were yet no folks to supply. And others. Some were owners and investors. Others were simple riders, cowboys true to the vision of the west, riding for the brand, whatever that required, putting up with the hardships and thriving under the challenge. They were pacesetters. Explorers in their own right. Individuals that could be depended on.

And what of those not in ranching circles? There have been men and women rising to the call from every culture and time. Did anyone understand the true dilemma of the Metis the way Louis Riel did? And was anyone in the West to be more abused by the eastern historians, who saw the Metis only as a problem to be pushed aside?

For the Blackfoot Natives the name Crowfoot was second to none. Chief. And Chief of Chiefs. A man born for the times he found himself in, greatly respected by Native and settler alike.

John Ware knew all the early cattlemen and settlers. Had worked with them all. Had earned the respect of them all. And with his move to new grass, he knew he might never see many of them again.

John Ware, the first black man to ride the Alberta grass was there from the start. He knew and had gained the respect of all the early cattlemen.

Men who never before considered working with, or befriending a black man found themselves relying on this man's knowledge of cattle and horses, and his understanding of the land and conditions. John had been a leader from the start, although as often as not he led from behind, because that was the place of the black man in those early years.

From slavery to being a contemporary of the great ones in early Alberta ranching circles, had been a long and sometimes wearying trail for this black man. He didn't know it then, but he would be vindicated, with his name standing out in the history of the grasslands.

And now he was leading again. Leading because he had to, accepting that he had no real choice. Leading his family and those who would follow, to another new land, in a drier and less hospitable grassland, perfect for cattle but, until river water could be directed onto the land, not for cropping.

CHAPTER 31

Reluctantly, John and Millie accepted an offer on the Ware Ranch property and started loading the wagon. With two friends as helpers, John gathered up the animals: the cattle, cows with calves at foot, yearlings, bulls, the horse remuda, and his beloved dogs.

Millie took the seat on the wagon with young Nettie sitting tightly against her. John passed her the reins. She would handle the team, although she wasn't completely secure with the task. She was not comfortable riding anymore either. Since her first pregnancy she had largely avoided horses. John had trouble understanding the change in her, but she held to her position.

Now, on the long trip to the new ranch site in Eastern Alberta the children would take turns sitting on the spring seat with their mother and lying or playing in the blanketed space behind the seat, set aside just for that purpose.

Without waiting for directions from John or anyone else, she slapped the reins on the horses' rumps and the trip began. Reaching the top of the hill above their little house she was tempted to look back one more time, but she couldn't do it. She wasn't sure she would see much through the stream of tears in her eyes anyway.

Frontier ranching was a good life but never an easy one. And as much as she hated the move, she had to face reality. Their little Ware Ranch that she had come to love and where their children had been born was being squeezed out of the Sheep Creek country.

Dig in, hang on and get it done. That was the way of the frontier. Millie wasn't sure it would ever change. Through his efforts over the years, John had overcome the disadvantages of race and relative poverty, but he couldn't overcome the changes taking place all around him. No one could stop the tide of newcomers. What John was leading his family away from was not a tide of ocean water, it was a tide of humanity. A tide that had proven to be unrelenting. Millie slapped the team to get them to step out and cover more ground, telling herself that they had overcome before, they could do it again.

CHAPTER 32

John yawned and stretched and rose to his feet. With just the slimmest skim of pink on the eastern horizon he knew that the sunrise would soon take over the darkness now enveloping the city of Calgary. Patiently, he had waited for this moment. He had stayed awake all night, while the others slept, waiting for what he had come to believe was his only chance of solving the problem that confronted him. That opportunity would come with the dawn of the new day. Quietly he went from bed to bed, awakening Millie and the children and then the small crew.

He couldn't do what he planned in the darkness of night. But he didn't want full daylight either. Now. Now was the time. The job had to be done now. The cattle, as if knowing that the time to walk had come, rose one by one and stretched the night's chill from their bones. A few wandered down to the river to drink. Another few sought out a nibble of grass, although the camping spot had been mostly grazed off the night before.

Hoping for silence, or as close to silence as could be attained, John led in the staked-out team. There were no bells on the harness so there was little noise in preparing the geldings for their day's work. With no thought of breakfast, Millie, still fighting off sleep, climbed to the spring seat and took up the reins while John lifted the children, one by one, into the spot left for them on the wagon. With hardly a break, they settled back into sleep. Nettie, the oldest, took up the seat beside her mother,

The plan had been discussed and settled on in the evening. Everyone knew what to do. They also knew they were going directly against the word of the police who had threatened harsh punishment if they didn't swim their animals off the City of Calgary property.

"Not one hoof is to encroach on that bridge. Not one. You get your herd out of here and don't come back, or you'll answer to me."

At that point, John was more concerned about his animals and his family than he was about one policeman, who just might be making up the rules as he went along.

John looked over the bedgrounds. The cowboys were ready. The remuda stood more or less steady. The cattle were bunched. John hoped they would remain quiet. Millie was ready. She would lead out.

At John's silent signal she slapped the rumps of the team with the reins and began the day's adventure. If all went well, they would be on the other side of the rickety wooden bridge and out of town before anyone knew what they were doing. If something went wrong, men, horses and cattle might be swimming among the debris of a broken bridge.

The camp was about one quarter mile from the crossing. Millie nervously pointed the team in that direction and, without slowing or stopping, with determination, and convinced that her husband's assessment of the situation was correct, moved them right onto the forbidden structure. It was far too late to wonder about the rightness of, or wrongness of, the decisions taken. The facts were right in front of them all.

The cattle were here and the land they needed to reach was over there. Between those two points lay the Bow River, not a big river in normal times but when swollen with rain runoff, as it was currently, a formidable barrier for cattle and horses alike. It would be out of the question to even contemplate having the team and wagon stepping into the roiling water.

Once on the bridge, Millie moved ahead with a steady pace. The team showed some nervousness as their hooves shook echoes off the wooden planking, but they kept pulling. No other weight would be added to the burden she was placing on the wooden structure until she was safely on the other side.

John studied the slight sway in the bridge as the wagon moved forward and satisfied himself that it would hold. Would it hold for the cattle and remuda? Within the next half hour, he would have an answer to that question.

The horses were held back until Millie was safely on the other side. She had been instructed to keep going, to move across the bridge as quickly as she could without running the horses and to move well away from the river once she was on the other side.

Once started, there was no possibility of stopping, or even hesitating. If an acceptable location presented itself once she was above and past the rolling, grassy riverbanks, Millie would stop and, leaving the team in harness, stake them where they could graze. She would then try to get a fire started and coffee boiling. The older kids would scout for wood. Soon breakfast would be ready. But unless the riders managed to move the cattle across the bridge, she might find herself with no takers for the food.

Her concerns were soon settled. It appeared that she would have mouths to feed. As she was urging the team up the slope on the north riverbank, she risked one quick glance back. One rider trotted into Millie's view, leading the loose horses. He held the remuda back, only bringing them on slowly, to allow Millie to get her wagon safely ahead. To run loose horses past a team could cause all kinds of unwelcome outcomes.

He followed the wagon to the top of the slope and settled the animals onto good grass, a decent distance from the wagon and the kids. From where Millie had stopped the wagon, a short row of small houses could be seen and a trail of sorts leading north, out of the settled area.

Seeing that the remuda appeared to be content, the rider trusted them to stay where they were, while he rode back to the bridge to see what he could do to help with the cattle. When he arrived, the first of the herd were just stepping off the creaking, swaying structure. The sounds of groaning and cracking were shocking in the morning's air. But the men kept pushing, and the cattle kept walking. There was no sign of any policemen. A couple of men heading to work stopped and watched. When one of them pointed and laughed and then waved in a friendly manner to John, it seemed obvious neither had any intentions of shouting for the police.

Breaking into the stream of arriving cattle the rider who had led the remuda pointed the herd to good grass about one quarter mile past Millie's chosen camp spot. Millie saw them coming and quickly scooted the kids back into the wagon, away from any risk from horns or hooves.

John was the last to emerge from the bridge. There had been none of the shouting from the riders or bellowing of the animals that accompanied the typical movement of cattle. There was no sign that they had awakened any of the good folks of Calgary. Without giving it much thought, happy to have the ordeal behind him, John exhaled a huge sigh of relief when his horse stepped onto solid ground. He silently chuckled to himself when he remembered that the policeman had insisted that he get his cattle out of Calgary and not bring them back.

"Well, Mr. Policeman. We not be com'n back."

With his eyes always on the job that needed doing, John pushed his horse up to a couple of lagging steers and urged them along.

They had broken the law, if law there really was, and John was still not too sure of that. In such a small settlement, normally demonstrating little in the way of formality, it was quite possible that the constable had simply taken it upon himself to forbid the crossing.

The creaking and cracking of timbers and joints had been a worry. John's original intention was to spread the animals out further but to do that effectively he would have needed more riders. As it was, the cattle followed nose to tail, in pairs and sometimes three abreast, with virtually no gaps between them. There was little doubt that the combined weight of cattle, horses and men was a severe test of the amateur engineering skills of the bridge builders.

Unless someone took offence at the steady trail of horse and cattle droppings on the bridge, there was no visible sign of trouble left behind by the people or animals of the

Ware Ranch.

John took the whole thing as just another new day. One more challenge faced. One small victory won. There would be many more to come.

Now, safely on the north side of the Bow River, the only obstacle between where they were and where they were going was space. Miles. Distance. Hopefully, they could cover that distance in a week or less.

CHAPTER 33

Every man makes mistakes on his pathway through life. Some mistakes are small and easily overcome and, over time, to forget. Others are larger, lifechanging, grafting in a memory that will last a generation or more. John was no better and no worse than others in his decision making.

Years before, even though John had been welcomed at even the largest of ranches, and valued for his knowledge of cattle and horses, he was recognized as having a wandering eye and a loose foot. He had left several good ranching jobs, moving on where others could see no clear purpose in the moves. But that John himself could see an advantage was enough. He did what he believed would best ease the way into the future he was planning for himself. Later, after his marriage, he made the decisions he believed were best for Millie and the children, and for the future of the Ware Ranch.

With a new Red Deer River ranch site chosen, and the animals settled onto the good, short grass graze, John and his friends turned to getting a cabin up and livable. Better quarters would follow as opportunity allowed but the first order of business was to get the family under a dependable roof.

The results of their work would not inspire pride of accomplishment, except when it was realized that none of them were builders. But before long the family was able to move into the new, modest, quarters.

But trouble loomed. Millie wasn't feeling well. This pregnancy wasn't like the others had been.

She had been carrying the child when they decided to make the move to the Red Deer River country. She held that knowledge back from John until they had reached their destination. With the completion of the cabin, Millie quietly told John about the expected arrival of a new baby. As always, excited with that news, John drove himself harder than ever.

Pregnancy was not new or mysterious to her. She felt no real fear. But along with the anticipation of another blessing, was the concern about being miles from any assistance at the birthing. John and Millie lived at a time in which medical knowledge had not advanced far beyond its primitive beginnings. Doctors were few in the newly settling land. Real medical knowledge was slim to scant. Only the larger centers could boast a hospital.

Altogether too often, a simple matter like a cut from an axe or a knife would lead to infection, and often, death. Diseases that would one day be eradicated through medical knowledge, ran rampant through the countryside, proving to be as communicable as smallpox had been to the Natives. Home remedies abounded, some based on workable experience and some on ignorance and fear. It was a challenging time in history for settlers; perhaps, especially, for mothers and children. Many a child was to find a final resting place on a hillside beside a lonely homestead. The cemeteries behind the town churches were to hold a heartbreaking number of folks who died far too young. Difficult births and the loss of a child were altogether too common. It was a rare family that escaped suffering and loss.

As was largely in keeping with the culture of the day, John had little to do with the raising of the family, and nothing at all to do with the delivery of a newborn. He was quite content to leave women's matters to the women. And there could be no doubt, childbirth and the issues surrounding it, were most certainly a woman's matter.

Millie, knowledgeable in the matter of giving birth, and the possible complications, wanted to be closer to a doctor's care. And closer to other female assistance. None of that was available anywhere near the new Ware Ranch beside the Red Deer River.

"John, I wish to visit my parents. The baby is due soon and I can't face giving birth miles from a doctor or female assistance. If the children and I took the train to Blairmore it would be a fun adventure for the kids, and I would be near a doctor and hospital. And with no one under foot, you would be free to complete the cabin while we are away."

John was a few moments in answering but finally gathered his thoughts.

"Millie girl, dat be a good idea. I check over de wagon dis even'n and we make de trip in de morn'n to de rail station. I work on de cabin and watch over de cows while you away. You visit wit your Mama and Papa and, come by n by, you be com'n home wit de new baby child."

"Are you really alright with that, John?"

"Girl, I say it and dat be de truth. I be here wait'n for you and de new baby, if I don't kill myself wit' de cook'n."

"Well, John, it's certainly true that you lack something in the preparation of food. But you lived all those years alone, cooking for yourself. I should imagine that you can keep from starving for a few weeks."

The trip was made, and the family enjoyed their weeks with the grandparents. But when John drove the wagon to Medicine Hat to pick the family up, there was no new baby nestling in its mother's arms. Before she had even finished stepping down the passenger car stairs to the platform, Millie could see the question on John's face. She hurt for him as she watched his lips moving with unasked questions. While still standing on the station platform, with all the noise of the reuniting families and the puffing steam engine, she stepped close to be heard and said, "Oh, John. We lost the baby. The poor little tike only lived a few hours and was gone. I'm thinking God wanted another angel just to brighten things up a bit. This time He chose a black angel. I'm so sorry, John. I've wept and cried. So have the kids, and, of course, my parents. But none of that will bring back our precious child."

John was stunned for several seconds before he finally got his wits about him.

"Dat be sad news for sure, Millie girl. We can talk more about dis when we be alone.

But I's sure happy to have you home anyway. You and de children. Do you be alright? You weren't sick or hurt with de birth'n?"

"It was a difficult birthing, John, but I'm fine now. I'm not happy with the outcome but really, I'm fine."

Moving his family from the established holdings on Sheep Creek to the banks of the Red Deer River had not yet proven to be profitable. But John was convinced they had made the correct decision and that time would be on their side, as the herd grew with successful calving. They were comfortable enough in their new cabin, although a bit on the crowded side. And John loved the fact that they could spread their herd out over the large countryside without butting heads with other cattlemen or homesteaders. In his quieter moments, John thought of those things.

Having awakened early, with the dark of night obscuring a menace that John had somehow felt creeping into the dark room, he found himself in an almost frantic rush to save his family, and as many of their possessions as possible. He didn't have time to sort out the situation or to chastise himself for the choice that had put them all into such peril. There would be time enough for that later. It was certainly true that he should have known better. And the men that helped him build his cabin on the banks of the Red Deer River should probably have at least offered a warning.

John was no stranger to the risks and challenges of frontier life. He had seen the Old Man River in flood. He had stood on the banks of the Highwood River and wondered at the unstoppable power of even so small a gathering of water as was normally in that prairie stream.

Even on the pleasantly flowing Sheep Creek, which the Ware Ranch depended on for their irrigation efforts, the water could rise up and turn its normally friendly face away, while displaying its more aggressive side. John had personal experience with the hazards the Sheep could present, when he risked his own life to assist his new neighbor, a man named Adams, who had managed to get his cabin washed away and his small herd stuck on an island that looked so inviting in dry times, but was, in the current situation, awash in flood water. Perhaps it could be called a lesson learned, but then forgotten.

John had stood on the banks of each of those rivers, at different times, and wondered at the trees, dead animals and debris the swollen waterways had gathered up. He had watched in amazement as the water, rounding yet another bend in the serpentine path of the Highwood, undercut the clay banks and then pulled out great clumps of grass, brush and trees, tossing them about like matchsticks. He had seen new watercourses gouged out and followed as the flood waters found an easier route, altering the very path of the river, leaving the older watercourse to dry out, and eventually grass over.

In an almost flat country, where riverbanks were shallow, the force of water would stop for nothing until it had risen, taking in the width of land that was needed to accommodate its additional flow. The new town of High River was to learn several bitter lessons over the coming years.

One part of John's mind was chastising himself for not making allowance for the spring flooding of the Red Deer River, while his main goal remained the rescuing of his family.

Not more than one minute earlier he had awoken from a sound sleep, ready for the day's work, and swung his feet from the bed onto the floor. Although dawn would soon be breaking, the inside of the cabin was still enveloped in heavy darkness. He could see nothing but a shadow or two. But he didn't have need of daylight to know he had just placed his feet into several inches of water.

His first move was to rush to the door, swinging it wide. Even in the dimness of the early dawn he recognized that all he could see around him was water. The Red Deer was on the rise and showing no mercy.

He turned back and shook Millie awake. Once her mind registered the truth of John's words, she was into her clothing and picking up the youngest child in less time than it takes to tell about it. With her boots in one hand and the blanket wrapped child tucked tightly against her chest with the other arm, she waded across the floor of her new home and out the door into the awakening world. With a short climb, following the path up the riverbank, she and the child were safe. Placing the child into the wagon with firm instructions to say there, she rushed back down the hill to begin the clearing out of the cabin. John had the other children safely at the wagon, with his own warning to stay where they were. Nine-year-old Nettie wanted to help but John, speaking as forcefully as he ever did to any of his children, put an end to that desire.

With the cabin still in semi-darkness, John

lit a lamp. There was no time for words. Both John and Millie understood exactly what was happening, knowing there could be but the one outcome. They couldn't miss the fact that the water was steadily rising. They grabbed anything that came to hand, carrying it up the bank to safety. Finally, with all the movable items rescued, John instructed Millie to stay with the children while he slid and scrambled down the hilly path again, to drag up whatever he could of the heavier tools. He was almost out of time. Clearly, the river would soon totally overtake the small homestead.

There was nothing more that could be done. The little family stood as close to the crest of the hill as safety allowed, watching as the relentless flow of water flooded the home they had, barely months before, worked so hard to build. As they watched, John thought he could detect a slight movement, a shimmering almost, in the structure. And then, he was sure. The cabin swayed on the foundation of boulders he had, with great effort, dug out of the ground and carried to the building site. It was but a matter of moments before one of the bottom logs was washed loose. One after the other the logs beneath the water were pulled from the structure, giving way to the unrelenting current of the spring melt from the high-up, and far away Rocky Mountain snowpack.

The logs John had worked so hard to cut and trim and shape into their new home, were gone. Perhaps someone downstream would snag them out of the flood and make use of them, but John would see them no more. Once the base logs had floated away there was little to hold the building together.

Watching as their new dream, and their protection from the ever-changeable weather was torn apart, there was nothing to say. Millie couldn't miss John's rising tension and emotions though, as his arm around her waist tightened to an uncomfortable degree. John seemed to be unaware of the firmness of his embrace. But as the building finally collapsed, with one log following another until, with a sad crash and tumbling, the remains of the structure were dragged into the churning maelstrom, her husband's unaware exercise of strength was more than she was comfortable with. She wiggled free and replaced John's embrace with her own, holding his hand in hers while her other arm encircled his waist.

Millie's dream ranch on the Sheep River was gone, sold to new owners. Now the new cabin on the Red Deer was gone. They were in worse shape than they had been when they first rode east. They were starting over again.

On the horizon, was a new threat. This time it was to the cattle, the very life blood of the Ware Ranch. Although John had seen no sign of trouble with his herd, the warning came from the NWMP and the Federal veterinarian. There had been an outbreak of mange to the south of Medicine Hat. Mange. One of a cattleman's worst nightmares.

A man can fight an enemy if he can see him. He can even fight the weather, to some extent, with shelters, stoves, and clothing. But how does a man fight a mite so small it can't be seen with the naked eye? John already had the example of not being able to fight a rising river. It could well be that this new scourge of the cattleman would spread north, threatening the ranchers along the river. No one knew what to do, although there were many ideas put forth by desperate ranchers. They would fight this scourge, using any weapon they could devise, even if the situation sometimes appeared hopeless.

The ranchers knew they must fight and win if they were to stay in the cattle business.

Blame was laid on the recently imported

Texas herds. No one knew for sure if that was fair or accurate, but in trying times the temptation is to lay blame somewhere.

John's best hope was that the winter would kill out the mange mite and that the more northern herds would escape the problem. But he would keep a close eye on his animals until the whole of the matter was dealt with and put behind them.

Millie didn't care for the Red Deer grasslands nearly as much as she did for the Sheep River based Ware Ranch. At the original Ware Ranch site, she could enjoy the wide-open view of prairie grasslands to the east, or she could turn and gaze at the glacier topped Rocky Mountains. She could dip her feet in the cooling waters of the little river on a warm day and enjoy her children as they, under careful supervision, splashed and giggled in the small pool John had dug out near the cabin. And, when the weather was welcoming and the sun had set for the night, providing the necessary solitude, she could take a towel and clean clothing and enjoy a leisurely bath. None of that was possible in the much larger Red Deer River.

The Sheep River, under normal circumstances, had carried no fears or risks with it on its path from the foothills to the open prairie. On the other hand, the much larger

Red Deer held some fearsome currents as well as the rumor of shore-based quicksand. The rumors were enough for Millie. She kept the children safely at a distance and stayed away herself.

Instead of the green, gentle, pleasantly rolling countryside along the Sheep, with the forested foothills rising behind, the Red Deer River country offered miles upon miles of open grasslands, and the mountains showing a mere outline of themselves through the distance, on a clear day. And closer to the cabin and upstream, a seemingly endless expanse of badlands, complete with weirdly shaped sandstone hoodoos. She had heard visitors talking about coal deposits upstream, but she had seen none of the evidence. The family would still depend on a large stack of firewood, as it had on previous years. John spent many hours each summer felling trees or scavenging dead falls, dragging them to the cabin. They then had to be cut to length and split to manageable size to fit into the cast iron stove. The big kitchen stove would provide for both their cooking and heating needs, but that required an amazing amount of wood in a cold climate.

And the strangest story carried to the new Ware Ranch by their frequent traveling visitors, was of the existence of dinosaur skeletons embedded in the sandstone. Millie decided she would like to see that but the chances of getting time away from the ranch were slim.

The one redeeming factor of the move from the Sheep was that John's estimate of the nourishment qualities in the short grass was proving to be true. There was no doubt that their cattle were doing well. The yearlings they had driven from the Sheep were approaching market weight. If John could find a good sale, there would be spendable money in their pockets. There had always been a bit of money. John was a saver, a cautious man with money. He insisted on setting aside what might be needed for an emergency, or simply to have assurance that they were not completely out of funds. Of course, Millie understood too, that John forever had his eye out for a better grade of bull or for that one special horse that he might have to purchase. She didn't object to any of that, somehow finding it amusing. She also had a mental list of things that could enhance their lives once that hoped for extra money became a spendable reality.

CHAPTER 34

Losing the cabin to the flood was a bitter pill to swallow for both John and Millie, as well as a traumatic experience for the growing children. But it was an experience they had all lived through and could, with time, put behind them. The fact that they were determined to make the new cabin larger and better planned than the original, somewhat eased the pain of the experience. Now, they had only to make that plan come to fruition.

That Millie would have the funds to purchase a few niceties like curtains for the windows and some books for the children, would work to lighten the time for them all.

Before the cabin could be built, they were living in the shelter of the wagon, with the sleeping space expanded by the canvas sheet they had turned into a tent, attaching one side to the wagon box, and sloping it down to posts driven into the ground.

John was spending most of his time at a riverside stand of spruce trees, a few miles to the west, cutting and trimming logs for their new cabin. He had taken a bit of food with him and was not expected to return before late evening.

Millie was surprised to see him pushing his mount at top speed, calling out to her as he rushed into the yard and swung off the horse. Seldom did Millie see her husband excited or demonstrating such great enthusiasm. John was more of a plodder. A man fully in control of his thoughts. A determined and hardworking man, but as a man who had spent his formative years in slavery, he was usually in no particular rush, knowing that most things will work themselves out if given time. But on this occasion, he was clearly not only in a rush, but he was having trouble holding back his obvious excitement. Or, perhaps, he didn't wish to hold back the excitement, wanting instead to see Millie as excited as he was himself.

"Millie, I be goin' down to de river. De Lord be send'n us de new cabin."

Millie had no idea what her husband was talking about, but they all rushed to the riverbank to see this wonderful thing that was happening. The river's spring melt had passed on to the east, pushing the last of the shattered ice sheet before it, leaving the water level close to normal. The river wasn't quite placid, but it was slow and calm enough for a careful watcher to see what was riding the rippling waves for a half mile or more upstream. There, plainly visible, and quickly approaching, identifiable even from the distance, were spruce saw logs. Dozens of them. Perhaps hundreds. How far back the drift went, was unknown, but as far as anyone could see, the river was clogged with logs.

No one man, working alone, could capture and salvage all those logs. But John certainly intended to pull out any he could tie onto. There, right before their eyes, was exactly what was needed for the cabin. Where the logs came from or how they got into the river or who they had belonged to were questions for another day. John had no knowledge of maritime law or the rights or wrongs of river salvage. But he certainly knew usable logs when he saw them.

After slipping his arm through a coil of rope and running to the chopping block to grab his long-handled ax, John stepped over the lip of the bank and half ran, half slid to the edge of the river. The bend in the river's course, right at that spot, would drive the logs close to shore. The riverbank, on the south side of the bend had been flattened by the centuries of flowing water and the masses of silt carried from upstream and deposited, as the river slowed for the sweeping bend. It would be perfect for use as a landing place for the salvage.

John was going to get wet, of that there was no doubt. But he had been wet before. He took off his boots and socks and waded in until the water was over his knees. Any chill he felt from the river was cast aside, hardly noticed in his enthusiasm.

Digging his feet into the muddy bottom where he believed he would have firm footing, he readied himself for the arrival of the first log. As the float approached, he planned out his attack. First, snag the log, sinking his axe deep. Even at the moderate speed of the river there would only be one chance with each log. He couldn't hope to get them all. Many would sail past, perhaps to be picked up by someone else downstream.

Once the ax was firmly embedded, he would use the leverage of the ax handle to bring the timber under control. Then snare it with a loop of the rope snugged around the butt end.

After that the hard work of tugging each heavy piece to a secure landing would begin.

As the first reachable log came near, he

swung his ax, sinking it deep into the wood. As planned, he used the ax as a steering handle, turning the log out of the current and towards himself. He then slipped the loop over the end and backed away, leading the salvage to the flattened shoreline.

When his bare feet slipped on the river bottom, he fell, soaking himself totally. Rethinking his first decision about the boots and considering how easy it would be to cut himself or cause a serious injury if he missed a swing with the ax or if a log ran over his bare foot as he approached shore, he decided to put his boots back on. If a day in the river ruined the leather, he would deal with that later.

Once he himself was on shore where he could get some grounding for his feet he started to pull. With an enormous effort, he dragged the leading end of the monster log out, anchoring it on dry land. The log was long, weighing hundreds of pounds. If they were all like that, he could saw them into shorter lengths. One sawlog would make two or more wall pieces. He could visualize the cabin going up quickly with this bounty from the river.

With the leading end of the log on the bank, John pulled it as high as possible with human strength, anchoring it on the dry riverbank where he was sure it would stay. He then, now with his boots on, ran back to where he had first waded in. His excitement from having successfully salvaged one log was growing. It was time to snag another piece.

Over the laborious hours as the afternoon slipped past, one by one the row of logs on shore grew.

While John's physical strength was the stuff of legend on the prairie grasslands, it wasn't unlimited. By midafternoon his arms were sore, his legs trembling with the exertion. He could eat if offered that option and he longed for a cup of coffee, or, perhaps, the entire pot. But there were still more logs coming. He couldn't stop.

As he was pulling one more log to its place on the shore, Millie was standing there, well out of the way. Glancing up, John could see the kids lying on their stomachs, their chins nestled in their hands, staring down from the heights of the riverbank.

As John settled the log into place and slipped the rope free, Millie said, "I wish I could do more, John, but at least you could bite into this beef sandwich and take a sip of coffee."

Millie was pleased when her hardworking husband quickly took an enormous bite of the bread and beef and a quick gulp of the now lukewarm coffee. He nodded his thanks, his mouth too full to speak. With a small wave to the kids, he stuffed the last of the sandwich into his mouth and waded towards the continuing bounty from the river.

Log by log he pulled and strained to the uttermost. As each small temptation to stop entered his mind he pushed it aside and splashed again into the river. Knowing the drift of logs wouldn't go on forever and realizing that he couldn't plan on this ever happening again, he pushed himself to the limit. And then past any limit he had reached before.

Only one of his captured logs floated adrift again when its trailing end was bumped by another log as it floated past.

When John could see no more drifting sawlogs heading his way he stopped, standing hip deep in the Red Deer River, watching. He was unsteady on his feet from fatigue. Hoping there would be a few trailing logs, he stood there until Millie hollered down the slope.

"There's no more coming, John. I can see all the way to the other bend. You had best come up and have a coffee and take a bit of rest."

301

John had captured no more than one in twenty logs. But even at that there was a goodly gathering of timber awaiting the new purpose he had in mind for them. These logs would never hear the whine of a circular saw or feel its sharp teeth as they ripped into the still green wood, forming it into usable lumber. They would never be cut and crafted into a fine town home for some banker or town official. Their future held a much more important task. These recently cut spruce trees would become the shelter for the John and Millie Ware family. In John's eyes there was nothing more valuable that this wonderful offering from the river could be put to.

As John looked over the logs he had successfully dragged ashore, he figured he had seldom seen a prettier sight.

Fearing what might happen over the long dark night if he left his bounty where they were, John made his way up the slope where he gave Millie a wet hug.

"Dat be our cabin ly'n der, Millie girl. We need to be thank'n de Lord for all His help."

With that he went to the corral and led out the single heavy horse he kept, just because he enjoyed having him around. To John's eyes there were few more magnificent sights than a full-bodied team; Percheron or

Clydesdale, or Belgian, when in full harness, heads bowed, big feet digging into the turf, muscles rippling with the strain of work, the load slowly moving. Magnificent. To John's eyes the sight was truly magnificent. One of God's great gifts to the pioneer.

And so, he kept the one big Clydesdale. As he led the gentle giant from the corral he said, "Time fo' you to git to work, big man."

The gelding was soon harnessed and, dragging a singletree, led to the riverbank. John had taken a light team down the bank several times before, so there was an established trail of sorts. The bank was too steep for a direct climb. Before bringing the light team down the first time, John had taken a long study of the brush and small trees that covered the clay bank, figuring out a shallow slope that would make the easiest route for the horses. Then, after several days with ax and shovel, he had a passable trail.

It was there that he led the big Clydesdale. It took some coaxing by John to convince the horse that he was in good hands and had a reasonable chance of surviving a walk down the hill. But soon they were at the bottom. Each trip up and down with the lighter horses over the past months had trenched out and established the narrow but well-defined path. Dragging the logs one by one was sure to leave an even more sculpted trail. A trail that would last for years unless another flood should wipe it out.

The first trip up the bank, with the log dragging on the singletree was an experiment. The trail wasn't wide enough for both John and the horse to walk side by side in safety. If John walked behind, guiding the horse on the long reins, he was in danger of a broken leg, or worse, if the log were to snag on something and swing off the trail, sweeping John along with it. The solution was to walk ahead, trusting that the log would bounce over anything in its path without assistance from John. On the return trip John swung to the Clyde's back and rode. After the first couple of trips the big Clyde had it figured out and didn't really need John at all except to hitch the chain loop to the singletree.

The last two logs were retrieved in full darkness. Millie suggested that the timber simply be tied off to some shrubbery and left for the morning. But John was determined.

"Dis be a gift from de Lord, Millie girl. De horse and me, we rest tonight after de work be finished."

With the last log safely stowed on the level

ground above the river and with the horse cared for and put away for the night, John, nearly staggering, flopped onto his bed and fell asleep. Millie lifted the supper set aside for him from the warming oven and covered it with a cloth. She would let it cool, knowing John would not be back on his feet before morning. She untied and slipped off his saturated boots and then his pants and woolen shirt. The underwear would dry under the warm quilt she spread on the bed.

A few days later, a rider heading for Medicine Hat stopped for a quick visit. He studied the long logs, laid out side by side, and laughed.

"Your cabin, my friends, will be the gift of a sawmill upriver, just down from Red Deer. A boom of saw logs broke loose when they left it in the care of a man who went to sleep on the job. Must have taken a couple of days to float down this far. I expect there's logs scattered for a hundred miles along the shoreline. Maybe further. I'm happy for you, but the mill owner hasn't had the best couple of weeks he's ever lived through."

As so often happened in pioneer ranching country, someone, John never really knew who, organized a house raising. Much to John and Millie's surprise, individual riders and whole families in wagons, those that needed more traveling time to get there, started arriving in the evening. Ranching neighbors from across the river drove their wagons to the closest ford and made their way across, their wagons loaded down with kids, bedding, food, and tools.

Millie stood in astonishment as people walked up to her, introducing themselves. The children, most of them never having seen a black child, hesitated at first, but before long they were all laughing and chasing each other around the ranch yard. Nettie and another young lady about her age wandered off by themselves. As John was showing some of the men his corralled bulls and telling of the gathering of the logs with the assistance of the big Clydesdale, he saw the two girls sitting on top of a haystack, their heads close together, giggling over some shared story.

After an evening of visiting and getting to know one another over campfire prepared food and an endless supply of coffee, each family staked out a sleeping space. The yard of the Ware Ranch fell into silence. In the morning, after a hearty breakfast, prepared from supplies brought by the workers, the men went to work with the tools, the women busying themselves with caring for the kids and preparing food for lunch and supper.

People kept arriving during the morning. Ranchers and townsfolks John had never seen or known before came to help. It was the long and proven way of the settlers in the pioneer era. No matter who was in need, there was help available. There were undoubtedly some neighbors who held suspicions, or at the least, mixed feelings about the races, and others who were unlike they were themselves, in skin color or habits. They were living in a time in history when travel was difficult, even though the rails spreading across the continent were making it easier. Most people had little if any experience of life, or people, more than a few miles beyond their home places. Even those from the east who had migrated to the wide-open lands of the west had, for the most part, brought their habits and beliefs with them. To say there was a general narrowness of mind and experience would only be expressing the truth.

It is quite likely that there were people sleeping in the Ware Ranch yard who had never seen or spoken to a black person before.

Further north, in the heavily bushed, black soil areas of the west, where the homesteads were filling up by the hundred with eastern Europeans, the Polish, the

Ukrainians, the Russians were lumped together and called Bohemians, or other derogatory names such as bohunk. Not enough was known about these modest people to truly consider what the term represented or how it could hurt the one hearing it. The simple, struggling ways of these misunderstood people were taken as a sign of laziness or of a simple, backward mind. But what was missed in the common prejudice of the day was the immigrants all-consuming drive to have their next generation educated. Organizing a school district was one of the first things undertaken in the communities.

The first generations to land on the prairies sacrificed all for the benefit of the next, and the whole of society was to benefit from that action.

The hatred for the Irish was common, with little background to support the feelings. Unknown, for the most part, was the history of the thousands of white Irish children and adults alike, that had been sold into slavery. The horrors of the potato famine and the mismanagement of the English overlords was either unknown or ignored.

Even on the Alberta grasslands, many of the titled English who had invested heavily in the ranch economy continued to look with disdain on the cowboys who managed their investments and who did the actual work required to make the ranch profitable.

That there were unfair feelings and suspicions placed on those with black skin was no real surprise. It seems that all through the history of mankind those same feeling had been placed in the way of any person or people who were different in some way from the majority.

Blacks were few in the Canadian West. John Ware was one of the first. Millie's family arrived just a few years later than John. John was certainly aware, after two decades of slavery, that life for Blacks, wherever they went was going to present challenges that weren't put in the way of whites. In his years of freedom John had accomplished much. Through hard work, diligence, competence and showing that he could be depended upon, he had won over most of the ranching community, becoming close friend with many. But the Red Deer River country was a new area. Even if there were other ranchers who had heard of him or met him briefly, most of those who came to the house raising had no knowledge of the Ware family, beyond the fact that they had lost their home and needed help.

Still, at the time in history of a still settling west, trustworthiness and depend-
ability were topmost. A man wouldn't work
beside another who couldn't be trusted. If a
man's riding partner, in the vernacular of
the day, wasn't "fit to ride the river with,"
then he also wasn't fit to partner with. John
had proven over and over that he could be
depended on. That alone had won him both
jobs and friends.

Somehow, these neighbors, strangers for
the most part, managed to overlook prejudices and tamp down their personal feelings. A neighbor needed help. That was
enough. They grabbed their tools and went
to work. There was a cabin to build.

As the work moved ahead, John and Millie both looked at the activity in the yard
with wonder.

By noon there was the outline of a sub-
stantial cabin laid out on a bed of foundation rocks that John had dug out of the
riverbed weeks before. There was much
laughing among the men, about the gift of
logs. A few riverside ranchers told of how
they, too, had snagged a few of the treasured
gifts from the river.

One rancher who had considerable experience with log work detailed two men to the
skinning of bark while two others wielded

the big, two-man crosscut saw, sawing the logs to the lengths relayed to them by the men doing the framing.

Although Millie was working with the women as they prepared food and cared for the children, she couldn't keep her eyes off the work of the men. Log by log the structure rose, finally reaching roof height. As the roof beams were raised and dropped into place she stood in amazement, never having imagined a cabin being put together that quickly. Or so well. Walking back to where the women were working, using a couple of wagon beds as tables, she commented, "I would have never believed it if I hadn't seen with my own eyes. I don't know how we will ever be able to pay you back."

One of the women looked up from where she was peeling potatoes and said, "That fella doing all the shouting and the giving of orders? That's my husband. He's never been known as delicate or diplomatic, but he does know how to put up a building. You might notice that no one is arguing with him. When my Kenny puts a building together it will be there for your grandchildren to raise their kids in. He truly loves to build things. He only keeps cattle to pay the bills.

"And, my dear, there is no pay back expected for this day's work. But don't be surprised if someone were to ride past and invite you the next time there's a barn raising or some such planned."

Millie had tears in her eyes and a lump in her throat when she choked out, "You just let us know. We'll be there for sure. My father is a carpenter. How I wish he were close by to help. He would love to be a part of this."

CHAPTER 35

With the cabin built and the yearlings sold, Millie had gone to Medicine Hat on the train, taking the children with her. They came back all fitted out in new clothing, and with a couple of bags of apparel for the younger ones. Winter wasn't far off. The way the kids were growing they each needed larger winter coats and bigger boots. As the children opened the packages and laid each item out on the table for another inspection, John's smiling comment was, "When I be small, like as you are, I walk in de bare feet. I never seen boots except on de owner and his family, and on de overseer."

Nettie, who was showing the responsibility of her growing maturity, as well as the self-assurance neither of her parents had ever known, answered with, "Well, Papa, we are not slaves. And this is not warm South Carolina. We get snow here and cold. Anyway, I haven't seen you in bare feet lately."

313

John laughed and ruffled her hair.

Millie had purchased two new shirts and two pairs of woolen pants, along with some new underwear and several pairs of socks for John. He had told her he needed nothing but still, he showed his pleasure as the kids tore open the packages and laid everything out for him to see.

With Millie having made whatever purchases she felt would enhance their lives, she said no more about money. She had confidence that if there was a need in the family, the money would be available.

There was no bank anywhere near the Ware Ranch. John stashed his savings in what he considered a safe place and left it there, undisturbed. Millie knew where the small metal box was kept but she had no reason to touch it.

Of course, all John really wanted was more land, more cattle, more horses, and more dogs. Comforts meant little to him. There is no doubt he would admit to raising cattle for the profits, but it was possible that the adventure of the thing might be almost as important. And beyond the adventure was simply the having. Or perhaps it was the freedom to have. Or, maybe again, the proving that he could do it, and do it as well as anyone.

Slavery was decades in his past but a thing such as slavery is never really in the past or forgotten. From having nothing at all or any hope of ever having anything that was truly his own, John had long ago moved into a world where he could have anything he was willing to work for. He had never quite lost the wonder of that.

No one in John's circle of friends or neighbors, in the present or in the past, had any way to understand slavery or the freedoms that came with his release from slavery. Even Millie and her parents, having been born free, had no sure way to understand what truly drove John as he grew his herds. He never came right out and declared "these are mine. Like the Ware Ranch they belong to me, and to us, to my family. I earned them and bought them". But perhaps the thought was there, even if subconscious.

On rare occasions John thought of his birth family. His parents. His brothers. His sisters. Beyond wondering where they were, he also wondered if they had found a way to enjoy the offerings of freedom, such as he had.

That John was an excellent cattleman and an even better horseman, was beyond dispute. When he purchased a new bull or a new saddle horse or rode off to break a range animal for a neighbor, Millie understood. This was her husband. This is who he is and how he is. And in the meantime, he never neglected his own stock or his own family obligations.

Millie, even though there was much she still didn't comprehend, took what she could get out of the marriage, loving her husband and adoring and caring for her growing family.

The single darkness in their time as a married couple was the loss of the baby. The memory of the lost cabin had dimmed in their enjoyment of the new cabin. The loss of the child would be a permanent blot on their lives.

But, in the summer of 1902, shortly after the new cabin was completed, all was to change, for the Ware Ranch and for all other ranches in the area.

CHAPTER 36

Millie was delighted to have the new cabin up and ready to receive visitors when the federal government veterinarian drove his buggy into the yard.

"Step down, sir. Welcome to Ware Ranch. I'll have my son ride out and bring John in. He's not far off."

"Thank you, Mrs. Ware. It will be good to stretch my legs. There are a lot of miles between ranches in this Red Deer River country. Perhaps I'll just walk around a bit and take my ease in the shade of the cattle shed while we wait for Mr. Ware."

With that, Millie went back to her household duties. Within one half hour John appeared, riding beside his son. The son was quickly taking on the appearance and riding prowess of his father. He even slumped just a bit in the saddle, as John did. The two Wares, father and son tied their mounts in the shade and turned towards their visitor.

"Good morn'n, sir. What brings you out dis way?"

"Good morning, John. While it's always good to see you no matter what brings us together, I'd rather have almost any other matter on my mind than the current problem. Mange, I'm afraid is the topic for today. The hated subject of mange.

"As you know, we fought it last summer on the southern ranges and hoped to have it beaten. We dipped a lot of animals in the Medicine Hat and Cypress Hills country but, obviously we didn't get them all. And those we missed have come in contact with others. And over the months, that malady has found its way to the Red Deer River."

John scuffed his foot in the dry grass of the ranch yard and pulled his much-worn hat from his head. He had hoped and prayed that what he had seen in his animals was something else, perhaps just skin dryness caused by a rainless summer. But knowing the visiting veterinarian would not come all the way to Ware Ranch if he didn't have good evidence to back up his concerns, John lifted his eyes to the other man's and said, "I see some dry and wrinkl'n hide on maybe-so ten animals. I be hop'n dat not be mange, but I watch careful anyway. I push dem animals away from de rest of de herd. I thought maybe-so I shoot dem ten and burn de hides. Maybe-so de herd not get'n sick too."

"I'm sorry to hear that, John, but I'm also pleased that you isolated the sick animals. That action may prove to be a help. But it won't be enough. And I'm pretty well sure that those ten will have spread the problem to others so shooting them would just prove to be a waste and a hopeless gesture."

"What we have to do, Boss?"

"The only solution ever found for this problem is dipping in sulfur water. That's hard work and time consuming but it has to be done to save the cattle industry.

"We have to dig a pit, John. A pit that's big enough and long enough that when we drive an animal into the hot sulfur water and force it to swim the length of the pool, it will have been thoroughly soaked. That treatment has proven to be effective in other areas. It certainly was effective south of Medicine Hat and around the Cypress Hills. The great majority of the dipped animals recovered just fine and are healthy to this day. The problem was that on the open range it is extremely difficult to even find all the animals, let alone drive them to the dip tank. Some of those big animals have been running and hiding in the brush and coulees for years. Those are probably the animals that should have been shot and burned. But that didn't happen, so here we are with another year and continuing problem. That some undipped beasts escaped and mixed with others up this way is proven by the fact that you and your neighbors are all reporting the beginnings of another outbreak.

"Adding emphasis to the need to treat the herds as quickly as possible is the fact that the federal government has ordered the NWMP to place a quarantine on the entire zone. No animals may be moved or sold, until this problem is brought under control."

John looked at the veterinarian in stunned silence. Finally, he said, "Dat be bad news, for sure. De ranchers got to be able to sell or der be no more ranches."

"As I said before, John, mange, left uncontrolled, will mean the end of the cattle industry as we know it, on the grasslands. Confining herds inside barb wire fencing would probably protect them from wandering, infected animals, but it would be prohibitively expensive, and it would take time. No, I'm afraid that until veterinary science comes up with a better solution, hot sulfur dipping is the only answer.

"There is no doubt that you have an

understanding of the importance of this matter, John. I was hoping you would. I studied a sketch of the area with the ranches marked out. Ware Ranch, with this running creek that could supply the water for the dip tank is the most convenient and logical place to set up the treatment. Would you be in favor of having the tank built somewhere close by?"

John didn't hesitate before offering his answer. "If dis place work for de other ranchers, den we build it here."

"Thank you, John. I was sure that would be your answer. I have a crew of men lined up to do the digging and place the forms for the concrete sides. I'll direct them here just as soon as I return to Medicine Hat. We have a supply of sulfur in barrels at the Brooks rail siding. We'll start getting them freighted up here right away.

"If you could stake out a site that would allow easy access to the creek as well as offer enough space, clear of your own buildings and work area, to move the herds in and out and not disrupt your own ranching operations, the men could get right to work when they arrive. They will come prepared to camp out and care for themselves. Mrs. Ware will have no additional work."

Over lunch in the cabin, prepared by Millie and dished out by Nettie, the men discussed the job to be done. After some small details were worked out, the veterinarian said, "Each rancher will gather and drive his own animals. They will come one ranch at a time, so the herds don't get mixed together. We'll do the Ware Ranch herd first. Then, if you could move them several miles away, there would be little chance of mixing with the others. We're hoping there won't have to be a roundup to sort out the brands after the job is done.

"Perhaps a couple of your older children could ride herd on your bunch to keep them from returning to their home territory."

John glanced at his family, knowing Nettie and her oldest brother would love the opportunity to get away from house and yard jobs and take on this adult chore. He wasn't in the habit of giving them responsibilities where they would be out of his sight, but perhaps it was time. He smiled a bit as he looked on their anxious faces.

"Sure. De children, dey can do dis. We be ready when de time should come."

John chose a spot and drove stakes into the ground, outlining the tank, so there would be no misunderstand when the building crew arrived. Knowing the small creek was not really up to the demands that would be placed on it, he started digging a hole for a catchment pool beside the creek bed. The pool would have to hold several barrels of water, in readiness for filling the trench once it was in place. He wouldn't open the creek to the pool until he had the catchment hole totally dug out. He would complete it with a couple of gates, one to divert the creek into the hole and the other built into the outlet end. He would copy the design of the simple gate he and Dan Riley had built years ago on the irrigation ditch for Smith and French. He grinned inwardly as he thought of Dan, a hardworking, but self-acknowledged city man, who, since that time, had entered politics at High River.

They would need a fire pit with a rock surround in order to heat the sulfur. Placing a high value on his own family's cooking and heating wood supply, he couldn't offer any of that for heating the dipping tank water. He would have to bring a good supply down from the spruce forest off to the west a couple of miles. Idly he wondered how long the little forest could last. Several ranchers were pulling their building logs as well as their firewood from that single source. It seemed unlikely that the forest could regenerate itself as quickly as it was being harvested.

There was a lot of work to be done. But first, the water catchment pool.

CHAPTER 37

Within a few days the crew hired by the veterinarian, to be paid by the federal government, who in turn would be looking to the Cattlemen's Association to pick up the costs, arrived at the Ware Ranch. They stood down from their wagons and were looking over John's staked-out choice for the big ditch, and the already full catchment pool. Their collective eyes next went to the fire pit and the large stack of wood pulled up beside it. The logs were still full length. There had been no time for cutting or splitting yet.

As John rode down from the cabin to welcome the crew, he saw several startled faces as they studied this black man. Clearly, the veterinarian had not told them anything about who their host would be. At one time, John had known that look on a regular basis, but that had been some years ago. He decided to say nothing. Let the men work out their thoughts or prejudices for themselves.

"Morn'n men. Welcome to Ware Ranch. I be John Ware. Dis be a big job of work you fellas be com'n ta do. Maybe-so you be need'n someth'n, you tell me. I do what I can to make dis mange problem be ended."

A big man, looking and acting like the boss of the bunch said, "I'm Festus Bench. I'll be ramrodding this crew. Looks like you got a good start here. Nice pool of water. A good start on the firewood needs. It'll all be a help. We'll set up the camp first and then get right to work. Might take up to two weeks to build the tank. Then we start to run the animals through. Not much we will need from you until that time, John. I'll call if anything comes up."

With a simple nod, John rode back to the calf pen and the work he had been doing.

John had trouble staying away from the work as it progressed. He had seen workers in Calgary digging basements and ditches with a horse drawn slip, but he had never used one himself nor watched from up close. As strong as he was, and as willing to work, he could see right away that manhandling the slip was brutally hard work. Hard on both the horse and the men.

The task was really a job meant for a

strong team. But after the first few passes, where the sod and the first foot or so of the soil was removed, the narrowness of the ditch meant that only a single horse could be used.

Starting at one end, the worker, with the reins of the horse tied together and slipped over his head, to rest on his shoulders, lifted the handles on the slip just enough for the forward movement of the horse to cause it to dig in, pulling out a few inches of dirt as it moved forward. The skill was in holding the handles at just the correct position so the slip would fill with dirt. If he lifted the handles too high the slip would dig in too deeply and the horse would be unable to move it. When the slip was full, the worker pushed down on the handles, forcing the slip to glide on its rounded bottom and lift the cutting edge from the dirt. He would than drive the horse out of the ditch to the chosen dump spot, lift the handles high, causing the cutting edge to dig in sharply and pulling the slip over onto its top. In this position, the dirt would fall out and the process started again.

Both the man and the horse were switched out every hour, giving a rest from this brutal and backbreaking work.

There was no denying the nature of the

work being done, but the skilled men and the strong horses soon had a ditch dug, narrow on the bottom, allowing only one beef animal at a time to pass through, and preventing them from turning around. To assist in the control of the animal, the sides were sloped, narrow at the bottom and widening at the top.

With the tank taking shape, the concrete forming was soon in place and the hard work of mixing concrete by hand was begun. A few days later, the site was cleared of the construction materials, corrals were built close beside both ends of the tank, and the fire was lit to heat the water and sulfur mixture. When the hot, odorous mixture was at the proper depth in the tank John was instructed to start bringing his herd in.

At the direction of Festus Bench, the kids had been holding the animals just a few hundred yards away, to have them in readiness. John had pushed twenty animals into the corral at the leading edge of the tank. From then it was only a matter of opening the corral gate and driving the animals one by one, but close behind each other, into the hot water. Men and animals both reacted strongly against the stink of the sulfur, but once in the water the animal couldn't turn back. There was only one way to escape; swim to the other end, until there was firm ground once again under foot. Then, a struggling climb out of the tank.

Although the sulfur offered a sure cure for the mange it did nothing at all for the attitude of the cattle. Most came out of the tank dripping with both sulfur water and angry displeasure. But by driving them into the corral on the outlet end of the tank they were given time to calm down before again being moved onto grass pasture.

In a moment of carelessness, as he was urging a reluctant animal forward, John lost his balance and fell fully into the tank. His head rose from the sulfur water and with a sputtering shout he hollered, "Throw me dat rope. I ain't enjoy'n dis at all."

When the first toss of the rope failed to come near enough for John to grasp it, he pulled himself alongside the leading steer and swung onto its back. Together they swam to the outlet end, where John was finally given a hand up, and out of the stinking water.

If he was carrying the mange mite on his clothing or in his hair, that few seconds in the tank probably put an end to the unseen enemy. He shook himself and walked a few feet away. One of the neighboring ranchers, who was holding his herd in readiness a mile to the east, threw several buckets of clean water over John's head, although he was laughing the entire time.

"I do believe you're cured, John. Millie could probably even let you back into the house now."

John turned his back at the laughing neighbor and the workers and walked to where he had his horse tethered. He swung aboard and jogged to the house for a change of clothing.

CHAPTER 38

The dipping program took many weeks to finish. When it was finally completed there was a bite of fall in the early morning air. The full and final results wouldn't be confirmed until the following summer, but everyone involved was convinced that the task had been completed as thoroughly as possible. The tank would be left in place, although it was covered over with logs and fenced off to keep animals and curious children from getting into trouble.

The dipping program had been dishearteningly expensive in both dollars spent as well as time taken from other ranch duties. Who was to bear the costs had yet to be sorted out. But if mange was, finally and forever, dealt with on the eastern Alberta grasslands, the costs would have been worth it, compared to the loss of the cattle industry.

John Ware's dipping tank, remaining in

place, was to become a longstanding reminder to a troubling time for Alberta
ranchers.

John, growing ever closer to Millie and his
beloved children, and realizing, with every
twitch and ache in muscles he had often
put to extreme use, that he was no longer
young, worked long hours to secure the
future of the Ware Ranch, and with it, the
Ware family.

The dipping program had drawn him
from his ranch building plans. He had
intended to construct more corrals, more
yard fencing and more shelters from the
wind, especially in his calving yard. He
would have to hold most of those plans over
for another time.

As late summer moved towards early fall,
he was putting in long hours, even as the
days were shortening, and the night skies
were enfolding the land earlier each evening.
The older boys were assigned tasks to help
with work suitable for their age and abilities. Millie and Nettie harvested the big
garden, preserving as much as possible
against the needs of the winter weeks to
come. John had managed to find time to
dig out a root cellar of sorts, although he
would have like it to be larger. He could

expand it in the summer ahead. The small underground enclosure would do for the preserving of potatoes, carrots, and other root crops, keeping them cool, but protected against the deep freeze of winter.

Never quite forgetting the heartache and unbelievably difficult work, along with the suffering for man and animals alike during the storms of the past, John wanted Ware Ranch to be in readiness for whatever fell their way. Remembering the starving animals from that first terrible winter on the Bar U, he had worked long and hard to collect his hay crop, even while the dipping program was ongoing.

Digging the pool for the dip tank water had given him an idea. He dug another, larger one, closer to the ranch yard, and well away from the residue of the sulfur program. Kept filled with fresh water that flowed under the ice that covered the stream, this would be an ideal place for the watering of the herd during the long winter months.

Evenings, when the work was done, were spent in the cozy cabin with the cast iron kitchen range keeping the space warm. Millie had been teaching the children their numbers, their alphabet and to read and write. She had purchased a few books on her trips to Brooks and Medicine Hat. During those family evenings John would sit by, listening as the kids, one by one, read simple stories, guided by their ever-patient mother.

If John ever felt a loss in his life or a twinge of jealousy over his inability to read or write, he never made those thoughts known, except, perhaps to Millie. He had been free from slavery for forty years. It would benefit no one or nothing to allow anger or resentment to overtake him now. It is quite possible that he could have learned to read and write. Mrs. Quirk had offered once to teach him. He couldn't quite explain why he turned down that offer. Perhaps he was afraid to try, lacking some self-assurance on things that didn't involve physical work.

As the family evenings wound down, Millie would read from the big story book a neighbor lady had given to her. A large pot of milk had sat, slowly warming, on the back of the stove. While her mother read, Nettie would stir in some dry cocoa powder and sweeten it just a bit with a small scoop of sugar. Each child was given a cup of the sweet drink to enjoy during story telling time. John ended the evening with his usual strong coffee.

In keeping with Millie's own family upbringing, she would often end the day with a reading from the Bible. Being many miles from town and with no easy way to gather with believing neighbors, this teaching was left to the parents of each ranch family. Those evening reading times were to be the children's only training in faith and spirituality.

As had happened on Sheep Creek, the country was closing in. More ranchers were on the grass, although they were not yet crowding each other off the available range. Here and there a homesteader, perhaps with more faith than wisdom, had staked out a quarter section claim, usually along a small waterway. John looked on with concern, wishing there was some way, through either lease or purchase, to secure the range the Ware Ranch needed for its growing herd. But the leases were not available, and he lacked the funds to make a purchase. Striking a big loan at the bank, even if such a thing were possible, was well beyond anything John was willing to get involved in. He was debt free and intended to stay that way.

The seasons that had been following their natural rhythm for centuries, for eons, moved from fall into winter and then to the time for calving. Following the calving there had been some sign of an early spring but in the first few days of May, when the snow should be gone and the herds again making their way onto the newly greening grass, nature again turned the benevolent side of its face away from the ranchers. A heavy spring rain turned into a snowstorm, driven by bitter prairie winds.

Looking at the calendar gave the ranchers assurance that the storm would soon pass, but it was not to be. The winds intensified and the snow continued to pile up. The cattle, with little to constrain them did what cattle always do. They turned their tails to the wind and started to drift.

The Ware Ranch was too far to the east to expect the warming chinook winds. The winds that did blow were bitter on the plains while the mercury in the big thermometer nailed beside the cabin door registered temperatures that should not be seen in May. Millie kept the children in the cabin and stayed in herself. She went out only long enough to milk the cow while Nettie gathered the eggs.

But for several days before the storm hit, Millie hadn't been feeling well. She had no idea what the problem was or how to describe the symptoms but, regardless of her assurances that she would be alright, John was worried. As they waited out one more day, Millie's condition seemed to be getting worse.

Before the storm had changed everything, the weather had been decent for spring on the grasslands and the ranch was well cared for. John managed to convince himself that the family and the animals would be alright if he was gone for a couple of days. He needed to find medication for Millie. Exactly how a doctor was to prescribe medication for an ailment that John couldn't describe well on a patient nearly one hundred miles away was a mystery. But the worried husband was going to try.

Riding to Brooks, he left his horse in the care of the livery and caught the train for Calgary. Somehow, between John's inept description of Millie's condition and the doctors intuitive guessing, medication was prescribed and purchased. John was ready for a night in a hotel while he waited for the return train.

The next morning all the news, arriving on the telegraph wire, was of the fierce storm that had visited itself on the eastern grasslands, centered on Brooks and Medicine Hat. The news startled John. He had to get home. He rushed to the station and purchased his ticket, fighting disappointment as the agent assured him that there was no earlier train. Accepting the fact that he had hours to wait before the next east bound train, he spent the long, waiting time alternating between sitting on a hard depot chair and pacing the floor, and the big wooden platform beside the tracks.

Finally, he was aboard, and the steam locomotive was chugging its way out of Calgary and east across the distance. Impatient and worried, John studied the passing landscape, half convinced he could make better time on a horse, which, of course, was not true.

The train slowed coming towards Brooks as the fierce winds were buffeting and rocking the passenger cars. The cold outside the windows had caused frost to grow on the insides of the glass, the way it was expected to in January. But finally, the whistle announced their arrival in Brooks and John stepped down to the platform, pulling his collar up and his hat down.

Rushing to the livery he went immediately to the tack room and came out with his saddle cradled over his folded arm. The livery man met him in the runway.

"Whoa down there, fella. You can't go out there this day. I don't know where you hope to go but you'll never make it. Your horse will die and, more than likely, you'll die with it. You'd best put that saddle away and go get yourself a hotel room, if you know what's good for you."

John pushed past the man and one-handed the saddle blanket into place. The saddle followed the blanket. As he was working, he swung his eyes briefly to the livery man.

"I got to get home. Got medicine fo my sick wife. Went all de way to Calgary for de medicine. My Millie, she need dis medicine. I got ta get it to her."

"Your Millie, as you call her, won't be getting her medicine, and will lose you this day for your trying, and won't know until full spring what snow drift you're frozen under, you go out there now. You listen to me. I know the country. I've seen it all before."

"I've seen de storms too, but I still got ta go."

John tucked his clothes in as tightly as he could and mounted the horse. The livery man, looking like he wanted to try one more warning, lifted his hand as if to say something. He opened his mouth, hesitated, and then dropped his hand, as John kicked the horse into the drifting snow.

Thinking of that first, long ago winter with the Bar U, when the men scattered out, trying to hold the drifting cattle, and remembering how far he was from the ranch when the cattle finally stopped their headlong, southward drift, he hoped to have learned enough of prairie conditions to make it through this time. Before, on that first big drift, he was a ranch hand, with just the normal expectations of the ranch boss driving him on, and the dumb beasts relying on him. Now he had a wife and children. He would make it through. He had to make it through.

Brooks was a tiny settlement. It took no time at all to leave the last small house behind him and head out into the trackless prairie. There were few enough high points or landmarks to see in that country on a clear summer day. On a day such as John faced, with the wind driving the falling snow sideways, getting into the eyes of man and horse both, a rider couldn't see twenty feet in front of him.

With no adequate clothing to hold off the cold or keep the snow from filtering into every slightest opening in his clothing, the ride home promised to be one of the biggest challenges of John's adventurous life.

Finding a landmark to check the direction against was a hopeless undertaking. The livery man was undoubtedly correct in his assessment. But John had done all this before. Millie was unwell. And John's family was alone in the storm, nearly twenty miles to the north.

John had always been sure of his directions. Even his previous owner, Mr. Akins, back there on the Shady Acres Farm, as he had assigned the almost impossible task of delivering a horse through a war-torn county, had said of John, "Don't worry about reading road signs, John. You've always known your directions. Trust to that and keep going west."

He would trust to his sense of directions now. But the horse was balking, fighting the bit and making no real headway. John was only patient with the animal for a few minutes before he gave up and turned back.

"You be smarter than ol' John, horse. But you ain't got no Millie what's in need of de medicine. I put you back in de barn. You be too much trouble. I do better wit'out you."

As he trotted the horse back into the stable the hostler grinned, as if to say, "told you so."

John swung off the saddle and passed the reins to the hostler.

"You take good care of de horse. I be back fo him by n by."

With no more said, the startled hostler stood with the reins in his hands and watched John disappear into the snowy afternoon.

With strength that had been the envy of many men over the years, and determination that knew no breaking point, John strode north, and just a bit east. It wasn't long before he knew his clothing was inadequate for the task he had assigned himself. He thought about this without breaking stride. None of those facts mattered. He was going home. He had medicine in his pocket and Millie was in need.

Step by step and hour by hour John pushed north. He saw nothing. He saw no building. He saw no light. He saw no trees. He saw no fences. He saw no drifting animals. He was alone on the prairie. With his head bowed against the wind and with each step through the deep snow demanding a little more from his slowly diminishing reserve of strength, he pushed forward. Towards home.

He didn't give serious consideration to the possibility of dying in the storm but briefly the thought flitted through his mind, *at least I be on de land what I love. Dis be my home. My home on de north grasslands. Dis be a good place for ol'John.*

Indeed, it had been a good place for ol' John. It was here that John had grown to maturity in his thinking, learning to exercise

342

his freedoms and growing with the country. It was here that John had found his own way into the cattle industry through diligent work and careful savings. It was here that John had overcome the early prejudice encountered so often after being given his freedom. It was here, on Alberta grass that John had become one of the more highly respected horse and cattlemen in the territory. And it was here that John had met and married his lovely Millie. This was home and here he would stay.

It had been a good place for the cattle industry too, and for many a rancher, large and small.

None of that was to say it was an easy place. It wasn't that. It had never been easy and never would be easy. But it was good.

Partly as a way of combating the elements through size and good management, and partly for financial security, the ranches continued to be amalgamated. New, aggressive and far-seeing men were moving onto the grass. Some came with funding of their own. Many continued to depend on foreign capital.

Only the big outfits could afford the expense of adequate crews for herding, fencing and haying. Only the big outfits could survive the losses that had several times devastated the herds from Alberta, and south to Montana, the Dakotas, Wyoming, Nebraska and even further south. A sudden winter storm could exact a terrible price in the lives of cattle, horses and sheep.

The ranchers were learning how to cope with the storms, but until those lessons were thoroughly learned, winters would be a challenge to men and animal alike.

Winters were a trial. Throughout history winters had always been a trial. Natives, Blackfoot, Cree, and the smaller bands, as well as missionaries, traders, explorers, and others, men who knew and understood the land had, on occasion, still been caught out in a storm, suffering and sometimes dying. Anyone hoping to survive on the prairie grass in winter had to learn to bow to the superior forces of nature, seeking shelter wherever it could be found. Many newcomers had learned bitter lessons when they ventured out onto the vast grasslands unprepared.

Knowing only a small part of the history of the grasslands, but with the thoughts of his life and times running through his mind, John continued north. The Ware Ranch was north. Millie and the children were north. And John was going north. Step by step, wading through the deep snow, sheltering his face as best he could with a turned-up collar and a tightly buttoned shirt, he pushed forward. His long walk could be added to the myriad stories of heroism, of overcoming trials, of succeeding against all odds on these grassy acres.

But even John's unbounded strength was being put to the test. Finally, after hours of walking, trusting to his internal compass, which continued to point north, John was vindicated when he walked directly against a barb wire fence. There were few fences in the area. The only one he could quickly bring to mind anywhere close to where he believed himself to be, was a homesteading neighbor that had settled on the grass the previous summer. He must have veered just a bit to the west. But now he knew where he was. Another five miles and he would once again be on the Ware Ranch.

Making a slight correction in his direction, he stepped out. To complicate the situation, as if the constantly blowing and shifting snow wasn't enough, a dull evening had turned into full night

As was common on the grasslands, Millie had placed a lighted lamp in the window as evening was descending. It was true that she put it there specifically for John, although she didn't really expect him on this stormy night. But it was more than that. A lighted lamp in the window was a common practice on the vast and sparsely settled grasslands. Many a traveler had become disoriented and lost on the broad prairie. A light in the window could be, and often had been, a life saver.

It was nearing bedtime for the children. The pot of milk was slowly warming on the back of the stove. Nettie got up once in a while from her chosen space on the floor at her mother's feet to stir it. It was Bible reading time. The story books had been gathered and put away. Millie still wasn't feeling well but knowing the children depended on her, she had taken her favorite place on the rocking chair John had purchased on a trip to town.

Engrossed in the story and the warm cocoa, they heard nothing, and saw nothing, beyond the room they were in. Any noise or movement outside would be covered by the still howling wind. The frost on the window glass would disguise the image of anything coming into view.

John saw the glimmer of light from a half mile away. Smiling through severely chilled lips he thanked Millie and God for the lamp and made the slight correction in his line of travel. It seemed no time at all before he was at the window looking in at his family.

Treasuring the sight through a clear spot on the frost ringed window warmed John's heart, if not his feet. Unbidden, he had a flashback to his time with Sol, the wandering black cowboy he had worked with on the Fort Worth area ranch, many years before.

Sol had laid some truths on John that made him think, and that added some direction to John's life. During a private talk the two black men had shared some things of their lives. Sol, never a slave, had less to overcome than John. His freedom had probably meant freedom of the mind as well as by law. John was only partway to freedom of his mind when Sol came into his life.

Sol told of his plans and then completed the story with, "Yep, you got to have a want in this life, John. Got to have a want."

That same night, after a restless hour lying awake, John started to piece together his "want". The picture wasn't at all new. But now it held more detail. Perhaps there was also more hope of someday actually accomplishing his want. It wasn't complicated, really. And it wasn't more than most men hoped to have. A few acres of land. A herd big enough to provide for him and a growing family. A good stable of horses. A woman. No, not just a woman. A wife.

The wife's face wouldn't come clear in detail. It couldn't be expected to. But he already had a name picked out for her. A private name. Not necessarily the one her parents had tagged her with, but a love name he would place on her himself. He didn't know when, or how, or where. All he knew was that he had a picture. A want, as Sol had called it. He had been saving his earnings since his first pay, back on the Macintyre Horse Ranch. It wasn't enough. Not yet. But it was a start. A start towards his want.

Yes, he had a want. Indeed, he did.

Now, looking through the frost shrouded window of his small cabin, he pushed aside the cold, and his fatigue, as he gazed at the beautiful Millie reading to their children. His smile came near to cracking his frozen cheeks. What he was looking at was all he had ever wanted. That and the Ware Ranch which he had been walking across for the past couple of hours.

"If you should be here, Sol, I be point'n through dat window and be say'n, 'der, you see dat? Dat be my want. Dat be my Millie and de children what she brought into de family. Don't want noth'n else dan dat. Yes,

Sol, I be hav'n de want and dis be it. What you see through dat frozen window is more dan dis ol' slave ever hoped to have. Jest wanted it was all. Not sure it ever come. And der it be. Ol' John, he be a happy man."

John backed away from the window and moved towards the door. He could barely grasp the door handle with his frozen and snow-covered mitts, but he finally managed to push the door open. Nettie was sitting where she could see into the kitchen. She was startled as she saw the door start to open. She reached to touch her mother, warning her that someone was at the door.

John stepped in, pulling his snow-covered hat off his head so the family could see who was there, and closed the door behind himself.

Nettie hollered, "Father. You're home," and leaped to her feet. The house was soon a bedlam of happy greetings. Millie hung back to allow the children to gather around. She was finding it more and more difficult to stand anyway. John hugged each one and smiled across the room at his wife. When she finally came into his arms, he knew again that his life was complete. All his wants were right there in this room. He thought no more of Sol as he relished the love of the family. He even momentarily forgot about the medicine that was in his pocket.

The storm was safely locked outside. Inside were John and Millie Ware and their children. It was enough. It was more than enough. It was their home, their home on the Alberta grasslands, and they were together.

Life, for any man, slave or free, is uncertain at the best of times. Between fierce winter storms, summer heat and drought, harsh living and working conditions, and an almost total lack of adequate medical help, it sometimes seemed as if the newly settled frontier invited disaster.

The spring storm in 1903 was only one of the many struggles John and Millie, and their Ware Ranch, were to face, and survive.

Whether or not the medication John brought from Calgary helped her condition, Millie recovered and went back to her many tasks as wife and mother of a growing family.

But time was not on her side. Years of almost continual childbearing had, no doubt, taken a toll on her. And in her weakened condition she was not immune to the many communicable diseases that seemed to take turns stalking the countryside, leaving in their wake, sadness and misery.

Many contagious illnesses were running rampant throughout the land. Smallpox, typhus, yellow fever, scarlet fever, cholera, measles, whooping cough, pneumonia. These, and others, were a constant threat, claiming the lives of adults and children alike. Some, such as scarlet fever, measles, whooping cough and pneumonia, were especially hard on the children, putting them, too often, into sad, small graves. There were no vaccines and little medical knowledge that could help the worried parents.

In April of 1905 Millie again took sick. John sent a wire to Blairmore for Millie's mother to come and care for the children. Even with her mother lifting the great household load from her shoulders, Millie's health did not improve. When there was no sign of recovery, John wrapped her warmly in blankets and laid her on a bed of straw in the wagon. He carried her to Brooks, where she was placed on a train for transport to Holy Cross Hospital, in Calgary.

Work on a ranch takes no holidays. John was needed at home. While Millie was in hospital, he stayed on the ranch with the children and his mother-in-law, working, and waiting for news, hoping all the time that his Millie would be well again and could return safely to Ware Ranch.

But it simply wasn't to be. On April 9, 1905, Millie's time on this earth came to an end. Even the best of medical care at that time could do little about typhoid and pneumonia.

The children went back to Blairmore with their grandmother, and John carried on alone. What he thought about or what new plans he may have formed for the Ware Ranch could not be known, and certainly never became a part of the public record. It is known that his eldest son, Bob, returned to the Red Deer River country and the Ware Ranch, to be with his father. He was ten years old at the time.

Working together to sort out cattle for the scheduled beef buyer, Bob and John were riding close together when John's usually trustworthy mare stumbled as she stepped into a hole.

John Ware, illiterate because of slavery laws, knowing little or nothing about the geography or politics of the land, followed cattle herds north, across the 49th. parallel and into Canada, where he fell in love with the Alberta grassland. He was among the first to arrive.

He had overcome racial prejudice, and made a host of friends among the cattle fraternity, being loved and greatly respected by all who worked with him, earning his place in the long list of pioneer cattlemen in a new land.

John had been one of the first to bulldog a big steer, holding it down for branding. He had seldom found a task his great strength couldn't match. He had fought and defeated fierce winter storms and had performed at fairs and rodeos with his riding skills and his bulldogging. He had ridden the roughest of the rough string and had started a successful small ranch with his own savings. He had been driven off the open range by homesteaders and moved to new country to start again.

He and Millie together had re-established themselves, once again, after the flood took their cabin. And now cholera and pneumonia had ganged up on him to rob this great black man of his beautiful Millie.

But he was still a cattleman at heart, and it was Ware Ranch cattle he was concentrating on when the mare he was riding stepped in that badger hole. The horse went down, and John was trapped under a thousand pounds of terrified, thrashing animal. There was no chance of escape.

Ten-year-old Bob bailed off his horse and ran to assist his father. The unhurt mare rose and wandered off. Bob could get no response from the injured man, so he remounted and ran for help. The neighbors arrived as quickly as the distances and the transport of the day allowed. They could see immediately that they need not have hurried.

John Ware was dead. The date was Sept. 11, 1905, a short five months after the family had said goodbye to their mother, and John had laid his beloved Millie to rest.

With the help of the neighbors, John's body was moved to Calgary. He was to return to the city in victory, in a sense. In the city where he had met with the worst of the racism he was to face in Canada, he had returned to accolades from businessmen, politicians, newspapers, ranchers, and cowboys.

John's funeral service was held in the Baptist Church, the same place he and Millie had been married so few years before. The moccasin telegraph that had so delighted Millie was in full force. Riders came from miles around. John's was the largest funeral ever held in that small city up until that time.

His pallbearers were among the elite of Alberta's ranching fraternity.

He was laid to rest next to Millie in Calgary's Union Cemetery, where their grave markers can be seen today, more than a century after their deaths.

During his eulogy in the Baptist Church, the Rev. F. W. Paterson said, "John Ware was a man with a beautiful skin. Every human skin is as beautiful as the character of the person who wears it. To know John Ware was to know a gentleman, one of God's gentlemen . . ."

The John Ware stories, and the accolades seemed to know no end. From wealthy ranchers to newspaper writers, to thirty dollars a month cowboys, everyone had a story. A few stories were saved for posterity. Many were lost.

What John would have written about his own life if he were not illiterate will never be known. That he saw it as a great adventure is beyond dispute. If he ever felt anger or resentment towards those who held him and his family in slavery, he appears to have kept those thoughts inside himself.

It has been stated earlier that John was a mover, seldom satisfied. It would be easy to second guess him and wonder if he might have done better by staying put, rather than moving from ranch to ranch as a cowboy. His move from Sheep Creek doesn't seem to have led to advantage for him, either. Millie wanted to stay on Sheep Creek. Perhaps John should have listened to her.

But for overall frontier wisdom, few would have outshone John. He advised that winter feed should be a priority for the ranchers. He warned against the breaking up of the native sod. He was a man of peace who tried to live that way. What his true feelings were about the racism faced in Calgary, beyond his disappointment, is not known. What is known is that he returned and eventually won a place of honor in that city.

John hated to see the treasured sod being turned under. Within a year or two of his death major irrigation projects were underway, which were to lead to thousands of acres of grasslands turned into plow land for grain and root crops. John would have mourned the loss of those acres.

John was known as a man who did what had to be done. When the cattle drifted during that dreadful storm the first year on the range, John drifted with them, caring for them as if they were his own. When a neighbor needed help, John was there. When the mange problem became severe, he put his all into the battle. His mange dipping tank remained, and could be visited, decades after his death. The cabin he and Millie built on the Red Deer River is preserved and repaired. It rests on display at Dinosaur Provincial Park, Drumheller, Alberta.

The respect shown in the decades following John Ware's death is seen in the roads, streams, schools and geographical locations named in his honor.

John Ware, an American slave who followed the northward moving herds, and found his own personal freedom on Canadian grass.

It was an honor to have had him among us.

ABOUT THE AUTHOR

Reg Quist's pioneer heritage includes sod shacks, prairie fires, home births, and children's graves under the prairie sod, all working together in the lives of people creating their own space in a new land.

Out of that early generation came farmers, ranchers, business men and women, builders, military graves in faraway lands, Sunday Schools that grew to become churches, plus story tellers, musicians, and much more.

Hard work and self-reliance were the hallmark of those previous great generations, attributes that were absorbed by the following generation.

Quist's career choice took him into the construction world. From heavy industrial work, to construction camps in the remote northern bush, the author emulated his grandfathers, who were both builders, as well as pioneer farmers and ranchers.

It is with deep thankfulness that Quist says, "I am a part of the first generation to truly enjoy the benefits of the labors of the pioneers. My parents and their parents worked incredibly hard, and it is well for us to remember".

Quist's heart was never far from the land. The family photo albums testify to how often he found himself sitting on a horse, both as a child and into later life, when he and his wife owned their own small farm, complete with kids and horses.

Respect for the pioneers, working alongside skilled, tough workmen, and learning from them, marrying his high school sweetheart and welcoming children into the world, purchasing land for the family to grow on, and riding horses with the kids, all melded together to influence Quist's life and writing. Over, and under, and wrapped around his life is Quist's Christian heritage. This too, shows itself in his writing.

Quist's writing career was late in pushing itself forward, remaining a hobby while family and career took precedence. Only in early retirement, was there time for more serious writing.

Quist's writing interests lie in many genres including children's work, short lifestyle stories, cowboy poetry, western novels, plus

Christian articles and novels.

Woven through every story is the thought that, even though he was not there himself in that pioneer time, he knew some that were. They are remembered with great respect.